THE CO

. . . when colossal multinationals collide with the combined governments of the free world.

The battlefields . . . the jungles of Brazil, the veldts of Africa, the training camps of Japan, and the streets of America.

The warriors . . . a high-powered executive who must devise a cover-up plan for the Corporate Wars, a negotiator who must determine the cost efficiency of life or death, a mercenary who's been paid top wages to fight and kill, and an outside observer who's trying to escape the corporation's airtight security.

The stakes . . . total power and control of the free world.

LET THE CASH WARS BEGIN.
MAY THE BEST CORPORATION WIN.

The Cold Cash War

ROBERT ASPRIN

ACE BOOKS, NEW YORK

THE COLD CASH WAR

An Ace book / published by arrangement with
the author

PRINTING HISTORY
St. Martin's Press hardcover edition published 1977
Dell paperback edition published 1978
Ace paperback edition / September 1992

ISBN: 0-441-11382-6

Ace Books are published by The Berkley Publishing Group,
200 Madison Avenue, New York, New York 10016.
The name "ACE" and the "A" logo are trademarks
belonging to Charter Communications, Inc.

PRINTED IN THE UNITED STATES OF AMERICA

10 9 8 7 6 5 4 3 2 1

This dedication is a
       Formal and Public thanks to
              GORDON R. DICKSON
       everything in a friend and mentor
       that a young writer could ask for,
       and more!

The Cold
Cash War

1

TOM MAUSIER WAS A CAUTIOUS MAN. DE-spite his daydreams of bravery and glorious deeds, he had to agree with his friends that he was one of the most cautious of people. As such, while it surprised everyone that he left his comfortable cor-porate job to open a business of his own, no one was surprised when it succeeded. Had success not been almost guaranteed in the beginning, he would not have made the move.

Still he had his dreams. He dreamed of being an adventurer. A secret agent. A spy. Lacking the dash and courage to be any of these, he contented himself with the small pride of being his own man and run-ning the business he had built as an espionage and information broker.

His day began at six o'clock in the morning, ful-ly two hours before any of his employees arrived.

This was not difficult for him since his offices were attached to his house. In fact, he could enter his office through a door in his kitchen. However, he never went into the office unless he was properly dressed. It would have been as unthinkable to him as walking outside in his underwear. The offices were another world to him, a world of business and of dreams, while his home was his home.

One could notice a physical change when he stepped through the door joining the two worlds. His home was kept at a comfortable seventy-eight degrees; the office was a more crisp and businesslike sixty-seven degrees. His wife maintained a modest and comfortable early American decor with a few tasteful and functional antiques in their home, but his office—his office was his pride and joy.

Stepping into his office was like stepping onto the deck of a Hollywood spaceship when the budget was both lavish and overspent. While his home was comfortably frugal, he spared no expense on his office. Electronic display screens and their telephone terminal hookups lined the walls as well as machines for recording and storing incoming messages. Gadgetry abounded everywhere, almost all of which he could justify.

His business was his pride, and he started at six o'clock sharp. He didn't require his employees to match his hours; in fact, he discouraged them from coming in early. The first two hours of each day were for him to collect his thoughts, organize the day, and pursue his hobby.

This morning started out the same as any other. Without bothering to turn on the overhead lights, he switched on the first two viewscreens and studied them carefully. The first showed memos to himself of items to be done today. They were either dictated at his desk into the memory file or phoned in by him from one of the phones in his home or a nearby phone booth when a thought struck him. The latter was done with one of the portable field terminals identical to the ones issued to their field agents and it always gave him a secret thrill to use one, even though the data he transmitted to himself was usually of an unexciting nature.

Today's data was as dull as ever. *ISSUE PAYROLL CHECKS . . . RECONCILE THE PHONE BILL . . . SPEAK TO MS. WITLEY ABOUT HER STEADILY LENGTHENING LUNCH HOURS. . . .* He sighed as he scanned the board. Paperback spies never had to reconcile phone bills. Such tasks were magically done by elves or civil servants offstage, leaving the heroes free to gamble in posh casinos with beautiful women on their arms and strange people shooting at them.

One item on the board caught his eye. *CHECK MISSED RENDEZVOUS 187-449-3620.* He scowled thoughtfully. He'd have to check that carefully. If the agent had missed the rendezvous because of laxness, he would be dropped as a client. Thomas Mausier didn't tolerate laxness. His own reputation was on the line. All of his clients could deal with each other in good faith because Thomas Mausier vouched for them. If a purchasing client didn't pay in full or attempted a doublecross, he would be dropped. If a selling client tried to palm off falsified or dummied information, he would be dropped. When you dealt through Thomas Mausier, you dealt honestly and in good faith. That's part of what you were paying him his ten percent for.

Then again, there might be a good reason why the agent missed the rendezvous. He might be dead. If that were the case, Mausier would have to check to see if the scrambler unit on the agent's field terminal had been somehow neutralized, allowing a rival to intercept the message and set an ambush.

Mausier doubted that this had occurred. He had countless guarantees from the Japanese firm that custom-manufactured the units for him that the scramblers were individually unique and unbuggable, and they had yet to be proven wrong.

Still, it would be worth checking into. His eyes flicked over the agent's client number—187. Brazil. He'd have to pay particular attention to items from that area when he went through the newswire tapes, newspapers, and periodicals this morning.

He was still pondering this as he turned to the second board. This board contained both requests for information and items for sale from the world of corporations which had been phoned in during the night. Again the items were of a routine nature. Now that the Christmas production lines had started, the seasonal rush for information on new designs from rival toy companies was dwindling. The majority of items were from corporate executives checking on each other, frequently within the same organization.

Again an item caught his eye, but this time he smiled. A corporation was asking for information on the design of an electronics gizmo that had appeared in detail in last month's issue of a popular hobbyists' magazine. They were offering a healthy sum. Still smiling, Mausier keyed in the magazine reference and coded it back to the requestor with the footnote "With our compliments."

There would be red faces when the message was picked up, but what the heck, they didn't have the time for reading that Mausier had. They were chained to a corporation. Better that they got a little embarrassed than if he let one of his agents sell them information that was already public knowledge. He had his reputation to protect.

Again he scanned the board, automatically assigning codes to the items. When his employees arrived, they would spend hours coding the new data into the computers, but he could do it in minutes. After all, he had invented the code.

Each item requested would be encoded with the geographic region for which information was available, the specifics of the information required, the date it was needed, and the offered price. Any agent could then step into a phone booth or pick up a motel phone anywhere in the world, and, using his field terminal, review all requests for information in this area. Similarly, any item offered for sale would be encoded with the general category of interest, the specifics of the information, and the asking price. The buying clients would then use their field terminals to scan for any items that might be of particular interest to them. This system allowed both speculative and consignment espionage to be channeled through his brokerage, with Mausier arranging the details and collecting his ten percent.

With relish he turned on the next board. This board got less use than the corporate one, but was always more exciting. This board was for governments.

There was a new message on the board this morning. It was a request for information. It was a request from the C-Block.

Mausier leaned forward and studied the request. Since the C-Block had gone incommunicado after the end of the Russo-Chinese War, no information had come out, but they were always buying. Even though it was known that their own agents roamed the far corners of the globe, they still dealt with him and probably other information brokers. Whether this was to obtain new lines of information or to check on data sent them by their own agents no one knew, but they were steady customers.

It would be curious to see how his agents would react if they knew how much of their data went to the C-Block. Buying clients were not identified on information requests going out to the agents, for obvious reasons.

The latest information request seemed innocent enough, but then again, most of them did. They wanted lists of any and all new hires or terminations for two specific major corporations in a given region.

It seemed innocent enough. In fact, it duplicated several requests they had made in the past for different corporations. But these were two new lists they were watching, and in a different part of the globe.

Mausier pursed his lips as he studied the request. The C-Block was sharp. They didn't do anything without reason and they didn't waste money or effort on petty items. There was something going on that they were watching, something that he couldn't see.

He studied the board. Two new personnel lists. In a new area. In Brazil. Brazil! The missed rendezvous in Brazil!

Mausier was suddenly excited. Abandoning his boards, he strode hurriedly to his desk and clicked on his doodle screen. He keyed for a clear workspace, then input two items. *Agent missed rendezvous. Personnel hires and terminations.* He leaned back in his chair and stared at the two items glowing brightly on the screen.

Thomas Mausier had a hobby. He never actually handled the information that the clients bartered for, but all the requests and items for sale still crossed his screens even if it was in the vaguest of terms. As a hobby, he put the pieces together.

You didn't have to see the blueprints of a weapon to know a country was hurriedly stockpiling arms. You didn't have to see the actual medical records to know someone was compiling a dossier on someone else. By combining the skeletal information that passed through his offices with the public data he collected from the incredible mass of news tapes, newspapers, and periodicals he subscribed to from all over the world, he could regularly second-guess the next day's headlines. So far he had successfully predicted three border skirmishes, a civil war, two coups, and several assassination attempts. He never did anything with the information, since that would be a breach of confidence with his clients. Still it made an interesting and exciting hobby.

He stared at the two items on the screen. They were probably unrelated. All the same, he would take the time to scan the current events public records for any items concerning either of those two conglomerates or Brazil. The C-Block was watching them for some reason and he was going to puzzle it out.

2

THIRTY-SEVEN IS A LOUSY AGE FOR A CORPO-
rate executive.

Peter Hornsby grimaced at the busy streets below
as he stared out the window of his office. He was taking a break after realizing he hadn't focused on anything all morning. Monday morning blahs, maybe.

Actually, the "window" was a viewscreen with a
continuous loop videotape showing on it, the corporate world's answer to the office-status scramble
of which executive got a window viewing what.
In his depressed, self-analyzing moments such as
these, Pete questioned his own choice of views. Most
of the other executives looked at a seashore or a
morning meadow. He was one of the few who had
the "fifty-seventh-story view of city streets" tape,
and, to his knowledge, the only one who had the
"night electrical storm over the city."

Was this a sign of his waning career? Was this all that was left? Deluding himself with illusions of grandeur?

He shook off the feeling. C'mon Pete, you aren't dead yet. So the promotions aren't coming as fast these last few years. So what? You're getting up there on the ladder, ya know. There aren't as many openings you can move up into. You're just upset because they went outside and hired Ed Bush two years back instead of moving you up. Well, they needed a new person to get the changes in, and even you admit you couldn't do the job Eddie's done. He's a real ball of fire. So what if he's a couple years younger than you.

Pete returned to his desk and picked up a piece of paper, staring at it with unseeing eyes. The trouble with being thirty-seven was you didn't have the option of starting over somewhere else. Nobody hires a thirty-five to forty year old executive expecting him to go places. That was for the young tigers like—like Eddie. If Pete was going to go any further with his career, it would have to be right here.

His thoughts were interrupted by a tingling on his hand. His ringpager. He grimaced. Dick Tracy was alive and well in the corporate world. He thumbed back the lid.

"Hornsby here."

"Yeah, Pete. Eddie." Eddie Bush's voice was identifiable even with the poor sound reproduction of a three-quarter-inch speaker-mike. "Can you stop up at my office for a minute?"

"On my way, Eddie." He thumbed the ring shut and hit a button on his desk. The wood paneling of the north wall of his office faded, giving him a one-way view of his reception area. For a change, his secretary was at her desk. However, she was covertly leafing through a cosmetics catalogue. He touched the intercom button.

"Ginny!" He was rewarded by seeing her start guiltily before hitting her own intercom button.

"Yes, Pete?"

"I'm heading up to Eddie's office. Hold all calls till I get back."

"How long will you be?"

"Don't know. It's one of his surprise calls."

He clicked off the intercom and started across his office. As he approached the south wall, a portion slid back and he entered the executive corridor, stepping onto the eastbound conveyor. He nodded recognition to another executive striding purposefully along the westbound conveyor, but remained standing, letting the conveyor carry him along at a sedate four miles an hour. Corridor-walking varied by section. Some crews walked, some ran in an effort to show frenzied enthusiasm or pseudoimportance. Eddie set the code for their group. Let the convey do it. We're smoothly run to the point to where we don't have to dash around like a bunch of panicked rodents.

Stepping off onto the platform in front of Eddie's door, he hit the intercom button in the doorframe and got an immediate response.

"That you, Pete?"

"Right."

"C'mon in."

The door slid open and he entered Eddie's office.

Eddie's office was not noticeably larger than Pete's, but much more lavishly furnished. Instead of a panoramic scene, Eddie had a moving opti-print on his viewscreen. The print had always given Pete an uneasy feeling of vertigo, but he didn't say anything.

"Make yourself comfortable, Pete. It's two sugars, no cream, right?"

"Right." In spite of himself, Pete was always pleased when Eddie remembered small details like that.

Eddie punched the appropriate buttons on the Servo-Matic and in a few seconds, the coffee hummed into view.

"That reminds me, Eddie. My Servo-Matic is down. Can you lean on someone to get it fixed?"

"Have you called maintenance?"

"Daily for two weeks. All I get is double-talk and forms to fill out."

"I'll see what I can do. What are you working on right now?"

"Nothing special. Pushing around a few ideas, but nothing that couldn't be delegated or put on hold. Why? What's up?"

"We've had a live one tossed in our laps, and I need that detail brain of yours working on it. I just got back from headquarters—talked with Becker himself.

"Who?"

"Becker, one of the international vps. Check your conspectus—you'll see his name. Anyway, it seems we've been picked as one of several teams assigned to submit recommendations on this. It's a chance for some nice exposure at the top levels."

"Who else is working on it?"

"Higgins on the East Coast and Marcus in New Orleans."

"Higgins? I thought he got dumped after his last fiasco."

"Just shelved. If you want my guess, someone's using this assignment as an excuse to dump him. I'd be willing to bet that whatever he turns in, it gets rejected. I'm guessing he'll be out by the end of the year."

"It's about time. Who's Marcus?"

"Never met him. He's supposed to be some kind of genius, but the word is he rubs a lot of people the wrong way. If he thinks you're an ass, he'll say so. You can imagine how well that goes over in the brainstorming sessions."

Pete lit a cigarette and exhaled thoughtfully.

"So our competition is a three-time loser and a loudmouthed whiz kid. If we can't beat that, we should hang it up."

"That's the way I see it. But don't short-sell Marcus. If he's lasted this long, he must have something going for him. There's a chance someone's watching for some real dynamic ideas from him. We'll have to watch close, and if things look like they are leaning his way, decide if we go for the kill or if we want to cover."

"How much time have we got?"

Eddie grimaced.

"Quote, as much time as you need to do a good job, unquote. In other words, whoever submits first is going to be holding up their presentation for the other two teams to tear apart. On the other hand, if we take too long, we're going to look like a bunch of old women who can't make up their minds."

Pete thought it over for a few minutes, then shrugged.

"If that's the rules, that's the rules. We play the cards as they're dealt. Okay, what's the assignment?"

"Are you ready for this? Our everlovin' communications conglomerate has got a war on its hands."

"Come again?"

"You heard me. A war. You know—soldiers, bullets, tanks—a war."

"Okay, I'll bite. What are we supposed to do about it?"

"Nothing much. Just keep a lid on it. We're supposed to come up with a bunch of ideas to keep the public from finding out about it, and at the same time start conditioning the public so that they'll accept it if the word ever leaks out."

"Are you serious? C'mon, Eddie, we're talking about a war! People are bound to notice a war!"

"It's not as wild as it sounds. This thing's been going on for nearly a year—have you heard anything about it?"

"Well . . . no."

"What's more, there are supposedly three other wars going on at the same time—one in Iceland over the fishing rights, one in Africa over the diamond mining, and one in the Great Plains over oil. Corporate wars are nothing new. At least that's what Becker says."

"So who are we fighting?"

"That's where it gets a bit tricky. We're up against one of the biggest oil companies in the world."

"And we're supposed to keep a lid on it?"

"Cheer up. It's being fought in Brazil."

Pete studied his cigarette for a few moments.

"Okay, I'll ask the big one. Who do we get for the task force? Our choice, or assigned?"

"Pretty much carte blanche. Why? Do you have anyone specific in mind?"

"Well, I'll want a personnel listing of anyone in the plant who's been in the service or lost a member of his family in a war; but there is one I'll want if we can get him."

"Who's that?"

"Terry Carr."

"Who?"

"The radical freak back in shipping."

"Him? C'mon, Pete. That kid's got a police record for antimilitary activities. What can he give us besides trouble?"

"Another point of view. I figure if we can sell this war to him, we can sell it to anybody."

Now it was Eddie's turn to look thoughtful.

"Let me think about that one. Say, doing anything for lunch?"

"Not really."

"Let's duck out and grab a bite. There're a few ideas I want to bounce off you."

The two men stood up and started for the door. As he walked, Eddie clapped a hand on Pete's shoulder.

"Cheer up, Pete. Remember, no one's ever gone broke overestimating the gullibility of the general public."

3

THE SOUND OF AUTOMATIC WEAPONS FIRE
was clearly audible in the Brazilian night as Major
Tidwell crawled silently the length of the shadow,
taking pains to keep his elbows close to his body.
Tree shadows were only so wide. He probed ahead
with his left hand until he found the fist-sized rock
with the three sharp corners which he had gauged
as his landmark.

Once it was located, he sprang the straps on the
jump pad he had been carrying over his shoulder and
eased it into position. With the care of a professional,
he double-checked its alignment: front edge touching
the rock and lying at a forty-five-degree angle to an
imaginary line running from the rock to the large
tree on his left, flat on the ground, no wrinkles or
lumps.

"Check."

This done, he allowed himself the luxury of taking a moment to try to see the scanner fence. Nothing. He shook his head with grudging admiration. If it hadn't been scouted and confirmed in advance, he would never have known there was a "fence" in front of him. The set posts were camouflaged to the point where he couldn't spot them even knowing what he was looking for, and there were no telltale light beams penetrating the dark of the night. Yet he knew that just in front of him was a maze of relay beams which, if interrupted, would trigger over a dozen automount weapons and direct their fire into a ten-meter-square area centering on the point the beams were interrupted. An extremely effective trap as well as a foolproof security system, but it was only five meters high.

He smiled to himself. Those cost accountants will do it to you every time. Why build a fence eight meters high if you can get by with one five meters high? The question was, could they get by with a five-meter fence?

Well, now was as good a time as any to find out. He checked the straps of his small backpack to be sure there was no slack. Satisfied there was no play to throw him off balance, his hand moved to his throat mike.

"Lieutenant Decker!"

"Here, sir!" The voice of his first lieutenant was soft in the earphone. It would be easy to forget that he was actually over five hundred meters away leading the attack on the south side of the compound. Nice about fighting for the ITT-iots—your communications were second to none.

"I'm in position now. Start the diversion."

"Yes, sir!"

He rose slowly to a low crouch and backed away from the pad several steps in a duck walk. The tiny luminous dots on the corners of the jump pad marked its location for him exactly.

Suddenly, the distant firing doubled in intensity as the diversionary frontal attack began. He waited several heartbeats for any guard's attention to be drawn to the distant fight, then rose to his full height, took one long stride, and jumped on the pad hard with both feet.

The pad recoiled from the impact of his weight, kicking him silently upward. As he reached the apex of his flight, he tucked and somersaulted like a diver, extending his legs again to drop feet first; but it was still a long way down. His forward momentum was lost by the time he hit the ground, and the impact forced him to his knees as he tried to absorb the shock. He fought for a moment to keep his balance, lost it, and fell heavily on his back.

"Damn!" He quickly rolled over onto all fours and scuttled crabwise forward to crouch in the deep shadow next to the autogun turret. Silently he waited, not moving a muscle, eyes probing the darkness.

He had cleared the "fence." If he hadn't, he would be dead by now. But if there were any guards left, the sound of his fall would have alerted them. There hadn't been much noise, but it didn't take much. These Oil Slickers were good. Then again, there were the explosives in his pack.

Tidwell grimaced as he scanned the shadows. He didn't like explosives no matter how much he worked with them. Even though he knew they were insensitive to impact and could only be detonated by the radio control unit carried by his lieutenant, he didn't relish the possibility of having to duplicate that fall if challenged.

Finally his diligence was rewarded—a small flicker of movement by the third hut. Moving slowly, the major loosened the strap on his pistol. His gamble of carrying the extra bulk of a silenced weapon was about to pay off. Drawing the weapon, he eased it forward and settled the luminous sights in the vicinity of the movement, waiting for a second tip-off to fix the guard's location.

Suddenly he holstered the weapon and drew his knife instead. If there was one, there would be two, and the sound of his shot, however muffled, would tip the second guard to sound the alarm. He'd just have to do this the hard way.

He had the guard spotted now, moving silently from hut to hut. There was a pattern to his search, and that pattern would kill him. Squat and check shadows beside the hut, move, check window, move, check window, move, hesitate, step into alley between the huts with rifle at ready, hesitate three beats to check shadows in alley, move, squat and check side shadows, move. . . .

Apparently the guard thought the intruder, if he existed, would be moving deeper into the compound and was hoping to come to him silently from behind. The only trouble was the intruder was behind him.

Tidwell smiled. Come on, sonny! Just a few more steps. Silently he drew his legs under him and waited. The guard had reached the hut even with the turret he was crouched behind. Squat, move, check window, move, check window, move, hesitate, step into alley. . . .

He moved forward in a soft glide. For three heart-beats the guard was stationary, peering into the shadows in the alley between the huts. In those three heartbeats Tidwell closed the distance between them in four long strides, knife held low and poised. His left arm snaked forward and snapped his forearm across the guard's windpipe, ending any possibility of an outcry as the knife darted home under the left shoulder blade.

The guard's reflexes were good. As the knife blade retracted into its handle, the man managed to flinch with surprise before his body went into the forced, suit-induced limpness ordered by his belt computer. Either the man had incredible reflexes or his suit was malfunctioning.

Tidwell eased the "dead" body to the ground, then swiftly removed the ID bracelet. As he rose to go, he glanced at the man's face and hesitated involuntarily. Even in the dark he knew him—Clancy! He should have recognized him from his style. Clancy smiled and winked to acknowledge mutual recognition. You couldn't do much else in a "dead" combat suit.

Tidwell paused long enough to smile and tap his fallen rival on the forehead with the point of his knife. Clancy rolled his eyes in silent acknowledgement. He was going to have a rough time continuing his argument that knives were inefficient after tonight.

Then the major was moving again. Friendship was fine, but he had a job to do and he was running behind schedule. A diversion can only last so long. Quickly he backtracked Clancy's route, resheathing his knife and drawing his pistol as he went. A figure materialized out of the shadows ahead.

"I told you there wouldn't be anything there!" came the whispered comment.

Tidwell shot him in the chest, his weapon making a muffled "pfut," and the figure crumpled. Almost disdainfully, the major relieved him of his ID bracelet. Obviously this man wouldn't last long. In one night he had made two major mistakes: ignoring a sound in the night, and talking on silent guard. It was men like this who gave mercenaries a bad name.

He paused to orient himself. Up two more huts and over three. Abandoning much of his earlier stealth, he moved swiftly onward in a low crouch, pausing only at intersections to check for hostile movement. He had a momentary advantage with the two quadrant guards out of action, but it would soon come to an abrupt halt when the roaming guards made their rounds.

Then he was at his target, a hut indistinguishable from any of the other barracks or duty huts in the compound. The difference was that Intelligence confirmed and cross-confirmed that this was it! The command post of the compound! Inside this hut was the nerve center of the defense, all tactical officers as well as the communication equipment necessary to coordinate the troops.

Tidwell unslung his pack and eased it to the ground next to him. Opening the flap, he withdrew four charges, checking the clock on each to insure synchronization. He had seen beautiful missions ruled invalid because time of explosion (TOE) could not be verified, and it wasn't going to happen to him. He double-checked the clocks. He didn't know about the communications or oil companies, but the Timex industry should be making a hefty profit out of this war.

Tucking two charges under his arm and grasping one in each hand, he made a quick circuit of the building, pausing at each corner just long enough to plant a charge on the wall. The fourth charge he set left-handed, the silenced pistol back in his right hand, eyes probing the dark. It was taking too long! The roaming guards would be around any minute now.

Rising to his feet, he darted away, running at high speed now, stealth completely abandoned. Two huts away he slid to a stop, dropping prone and flattening against the wall of the hut. Without pausing to catch his breath, his left hand went to his throat mike.

"Decker! They're set! Blow it!"

Nothing happened.

"Decker! Can you read me? Blow it!" He tapped the mike with his fingernail.

Still nothing.

"Blow it, damn you. . . ."

POW!

Tidwell rolled to his feet and darted around the corner. Even though it sounded loud in the stillness of night, that was no explosion. Someone was shooting, probably at him.

"Decker! Blow it!"

POW! POW!

No mistaking it now. He was drawing fire. Cursing, he snapped off a round in the general direction of the shots, but it was a lost cause and he knew it. Already he could hear shouts as more men took up the pursuit. If he could only lead them away from the charges. Ducking around a corner, he flattened against the wall and tried to catch his breath. Again he tried the mike.

"Decker!"

The door of the hut across the alley burst open, flooding the scene with light. As if in a nightmare, he snapped off a shot at the figure silhouetted in the door as he scrambled backwards around the corner.

POW!

He was dead. There was no impact of the "bullet," but his suit collapsed, taking him with it as it crumpled to the ground. Even if he could move now, which he couldn't, it would do him no good. The same quartz light beam that scored the fatal hit on his suit deactivated his weapons. He could do nothing but lie there helplessly as his killer approached to relieve him of his ID bracelet. The man bending over him raised his eyebrows in silent surprise when he saw the rank of his victim, but he didn't comment on it. You don't talk to a corpse.

As the man moved on, Tidwell sighed and settled back to wait. No one would reactivate his suit until thirty minutes after the last shot was fired. His only hope would be if Decker would detonate the charges, but he knew that wouldn't happen. It was another foul-up.

Damn radios! Another mission blown to hell!

The major sighed again. Lying there in a dead suit was preferable to actually being dead, but that might be open to debate when he reported in. Someone's head would roll over tonight's failure. As the senior officer, he was the logical choice.

4

"HEY, FRED! WAIT A MINUTE!"

Fred Willard stopped with one hand on the glass doors and turned to see Ivan Kramitz waving at him from the sidewalk. Forcing a smile, he waved back and waited to see what the son-of-a-bitch wanted.

He hated Ivan with a passion, and knew it was reciprocated. Their dislike for each other was not particularly surprising as the men were physical and cultural opposites competing successfully in identical positions. Ivan was a recent immigrant to America—some said a refugee from the Russo-Chinese War—while Fred was from a long line of fringe-poor Americans. Where Ivan was the image of a Hungarian fencing master in appearance, poise, and arrogance, Fred knew his rounded figure and rolling gait brought to mind a beer-swilling, red-necked cop. Add to this their age difference—Fred in his mid-fifties, Ivan in his early thirties—and the fact that they were employed by rival corporations, and it was inevitable that each saw his rival as the personification of everything he hated and fought against.

However, you couldn't ignore a chance to talk with the second-in-command of Oil's negotiating team outside of the conference room, particularly if you're third in command of the Communications negotiating team. So Fred waited while Ivan closed the distance between them at a leisurely saunter.

"Sorry to keep you waiting, my friend, but I did want to speak with you before you headed in." Ivan smiled through his accent.

Fred returned his smile with an equally insincere toothiness. He had discovered several weeks ago that when he wanted to, Ivan could speak flawless English and only used the accent to irritate Fred.

"No problem, Ivan. What can I do for you?"

"I was merely curious if your team was still interested in that four million barrels of fuel?"

Interested? Damn straight they were interested. They had forty fighter planes grounded until they could get reserves back up.

"I'm not sure, Ivan. I'll have to check with the boys. Why? Are the Oil czars loosening up a bit?"

"Possibly. I've heard a few rumors I might be able to follow up on. Just because they refused your first few offers doesn't mean they aren't interested. Maybe if you offered an exchange instead of a simple purchase. I have relatively reliable information that they might be willing to release the fuel if Communications were willing to share the plans for the throat-mike communicators currently in use."

Bingo! Those bastards wouldn't be so ready to deal if those throat-mike systems weren't giving them real problems. Time to twist the old knife a little.

"I dunno, Ivan. The boys are mighty touchy about those little toys. I don't think they'd be too wild about our trading them off that easily."

Ivan grinned like a barracuda.

"As a matter of fact, Frederick, the rumor I heard stated specifically that your troops were not to be notified of the exchange. You know, a little . . . 'under the table' deal between old friends."

You son-of-a-bitch! You want us to sell our own men down the river! You want us to turn your Oil Slicker wolves loose with those hookups without warning our own troops!

"N-F-W! No fucking way, baby!" He maintained his smile even though it hurt. "No way will we turn those toys loose unannounced for a few crummy gallons of fuel!"

"You disappoint me, my friend. Certainly my superiors are aware that such an exchange would require some additional bonuses for Communications."

"Such as what?"

"Unfortunately those figures are not available at this time. Perhaps we could continue our discussion over lunch?" Without waiting for an answer, he stepped past Fred and disappeared into the depths of the building.

Those figures are not available—damn! That bastard had the pat phrases down cold. In corporate jargon, he had just said, "Eat your heart out, sweetheart. I'm not saying anything more until I'm good and ready!"

Shit! It was times like this you hated being a negotiator. It was clear that the Oilers wanted those hookups and on their terms. And they'd get them. Ivan was far too confident not to be sure his offer would be beyond refusal.

The irritating part was that he had specifically chosen Fred to make his offer to. Not only did he know his offer couldn't be refused, he also knew Fred hated like the plague to give in. If Fred had his way, Oil could offer their entire North American—hell, their whole western hemisphere holdings before he sold their own men down the river.

But he followed orders just like everyone else, and if the Lord High Muckity-Mucks decided it was a good idea, he'd have to knuckle under and accept it. Ivan knew that and was doubtlessly glorying in it.

Not for the first time, Fred contemplated what Ivan's face would look like mashed to a bloody pulp. With a deep sigh he entered the conference room.

It was a spacious room, even with two dozen men in it. Fred smiled at the two groups huddled at their respective ends of the room, murmuring together and casting dark glances at their opposing numbers. He was greeted by the traditional assortment of grunts and vague waves. Really friendly bunch, this. But then again, they weren't being paid to be friendly. Like everyone else in the world of corporations they were paid for results.

The unfortunate part about being a negotiator was that no one was ever satisfied with your results. Everyone could have done better. Small wonder the rate of casualties due to nervous breakdowns and/or suicide was so high. Of those that survived, most retired young. Fred was the exception; at fifty-three, he was one of the oldest and most respected negotiators in the business.

"Gentlemen, could we get started now?"

It was the Senior Negotiator for Oil, it being Oil's day to chair the meeting. One by one the team members drifted to their seats. There was no hurry as it would take at least fifteen minutes from the time the room was sealed before the electronic detectors could confirm the room was free of listening devices.

Fred dropped heavily into his seat in the move so characteristic of overweight men. As were many of his habitual moves and gestures, this move was theoretically exaggerated to irritate and mislead his opponents. Anyone observing him would dismiss him as a harmless, slightly comical character—that is, anyone who hadn't seen him sidestep an angry longshoreman, then ram the offending party's head through a wall. Fred Willard learned his diplomacy not in a fine old university but on the streets and dockyards of Chicago.

"The meeting will come to order!"

Fred sighed and punched the buttons on his console for his regular morning stimulants. The tray hissed into view bearing his ungodly trio: a glass of orange juice, a cup of black coffee, and a cold can of beer. Fred took private glee in his traditional can of beer among the bloody marys and screwdrivers of his colleagues. He knew it irritated them, and an irritated opponent is a careless opponent.

"The chair recognizes the Third Negotiator for Oil."

Fred groaned inwardly. Those bastards! Why did they always have to start their damn cute maneuvers so early in the morning? The cuter the move, the earlier they started, and this one promised to be a beaut. With a grimace, he punched the record button on his console. Better get this on tape. He'd want to study it later.

The Third Negotiator for Oil was Judy Simmons, an attractive young girl fresh out of college. When she first joined the negotiations, many had ignored her, thinking her to be a "companion" of one of the men. This illusion was short-lived. She had proved herself to be as cold and merciless as any man on the team—maybe a little colder. No one could get a firm line on her background, but it was Fred's theory she had been recruited from one of the campus radical groups—the ones who execute hostages one at a time until their demands are met. Some of the men still speculated privately as to her availability as a bed partner, but Fred had long since reached an opinion: he'd rather sleep with a king cobra than let her near him, even if the opportunity presented itself.

"Gentlemen: as you know we have been engaged for some time in what is essentially a war game—simulated combat. This type of fighting was agreed upon in the early phases of the war as both sides sought to reduce the cost of replacing equipment and troops lost in combat. Through the use of IBM belt computers and Sony 'kill suits,' it became unnecessary to actually kill a man or blow up an installation, but merely prove that you could have done it."

Fred began fidgeting with his beer can as she droned on. He wondered where this history lesson was leading.

"The only condition placed on the use of 'mock weapons' was that if the effectiveness of a weapon was challenged, the side employing the weapon had to be able to produce a functioning model to support its claims."

She looked up from her notes to smile toothily at the assemblage.

"Of course, the close adherence of the mercenary forces to the mock combat rules may be at least partially attributable to the knowledge that at the first sign of flagrant violation, the old style of 'live ammo' fighting would be immediately reinstated."

A small titter rippled through the room. Fred wondered how many of them had ever been shot at with live ammo.

"So far this system has proved more than an adequate method for allowing us to settle our differences while keeping costs at a minimum. However, it has been recently brought to our attention that there is a major shortcoming to this system."

Fred was suddenly attentive. Behind the sleepy fat-man exterior he used, a little computer clicked on in his mind. Major policy change . . . initial proposal and justifications . . . record and analyze. Of course he was not alone. An intense silence blanketed the room as Judy continued.

"The problem, gentlemen, is one of logistics. One of the oldest techniques of military intelligence is to watch the enemy's supplies. By watching the amount of supplies drawn and the direction in which they are transported, it's possible to second-guess the next attack and institute countermoves before the attack is actually launched."

One of the closed circuit screens on Fred's console lit up, indicating an oncoming note from one of his teammates. He ignored it. No sense speculating on what she was about to say next when

by waiting for a few more seconds you could hear
it. Instead, he centered his attention on her presentation.

"Then, too, there's the guns and butter choice
where limited supplies are available. Ammo dumps
aren't bottomless. If you've only got a million rounds
of ammunition, you can't hit three major targets in
one night. You have to choose which one you want
the most and how much you're willing to venture
on the attack. What we've done with our 'simulated
war' is grant the field commanders carte blanche to
fight as often as they want, wherever they want.
Oil maintains that this is one of the major reasons
neither side is able to win this war. We've made it
too cheap, too easy to prolong."

There was a low murmur going around the room
now, occasionally accented by ill-muffled curses. She
ignored it and continued.

"Frankly, gentlemen, we're tired of having the
same quote, bomb, unquote dropped on us a hundred times in three different locations four nights
a week. To alleviate that problem, we propose the
following: to effectively simulate the actual logistics
problems found in any war, it ought to be necessary to establish a one-for-one depletion of ammunition and equipment lost in combat. That is, at
the end of each conflict, an accurate count must be
determined of each side's losses, and an equivalent
amount of live ammo or real equipment destroyed.
Furthermore, each side has to establish and maintain
ammo dumps, and 'replenishment supplies' must be
physically transported to the actual site of combat."

"Mr. Chairman!"

It was one of the negotiators for Communications. The Chairman nodded his recognition and the battle was joined.

"We might as well go back to using live ammo. This proposal not only duplicates the cost of a live ammo war, it increases it because of all the necessary records-keeping and controls."

"Not really!" Ivan fielded the challenge for Oil. "In a live ammo war, men are lost, and we all know how expensive they are to recruit and train."

Fred jumped into the fray.

"I don't suppose you have any rough figures handy as to how much this proposal would cost if accepted?"

"That all depends on how straight your men can shoot and how effectively they're deployed. That and how much money Communications is willing to spend to win the war."

"How much ammunition has Oil already stockpiled prior to the proposal of this change in the agreed-upon rules?"

"Those figures are not available at this time."

Fred leaned back and shut his eyes thoughtfully as the battle raged around him. That was that. If Oil had already stockpiled, they'd never back down from this proposal. They couldn't, or all the money spent stockpiling would have to be written off as a loss. Communications would be starting with a handicap, but one thing for sure, they wouldn't let themselves be bought out of the war. It was more than pride—it was survival!

If word ever got out that Communications let themselves be run out of a clash because of high costs, the other corporations would be all over them like wolves on a sick caribou. Everything would suddenly cost triple because the opposition would be trying to back them down on costs. No, they couldn't back out. And the accountants thought that costs-to-date on this war were high now! They hadn't seen anything yet. Fred's only hope was that they could stall accepting the proposal long enough to let Communications catch up a bit on the stockpiling. If they didn't, their forces in the field would be caught short of ammo and overwhelmed.

"Move to adjourn!" he interrupted without opening his eyes.

5

THE BAR WAS CLEARLY MILITARY, HIGH-class military, but military nonetheless. One of the most apparent indications of this was that it offered live waitresses as an option. Of course, having a live waitress meant your drinks cost more, but the military men were one of the last groups of holdouts who were willing to pay extra rather than be served the impersonal hydrolift of a Servo-Matic.

Steve Tidwell, former major, and his friend Clancy were well entrenched at their favorite corner table, a compromise reached early in their friendship as a solution to the problem of how they could both sit with their backs to the wall.

"Let me get this round, Steve," ordered Clancy, dipping into his pocket. "That severance pay of yours may have to last you a long time."

"Hi Clancy, Steve," their waitress smiled, delivering the next round of drinks. "Flo's tied up out back, so I thought I'd better get these to you before you got ugly and started tearing up the place."

"There's a love," purred Clancy, tucking a folded bill into her cleavage. She ignored him.

"Steve, what's this I hear about you getting cashiered?"

Tidwell took a sudden interest in the opposite wall. Clancy caught the waitress's eye and gave a minute shake of his head. She nodded knowingly and departed.

"Seriously, Steve, what *are* you going to do now?"

Tidwell shrugged.

"I don't know. Go back to earning my money in the live ammo set, I guess."

"Working for who? In case you haven't figured it out, you're blacklisted. The only real fighting left is in the Middle East, and the Oil Combine won't touch you."

"Don't be so sure of that. They were trying pretty hard to buy me away from the ITT-iots a couple of months ago."

Clancy snorted contemptuously.

"A couple of months. Hell, I don't care if it was a couple days. That was before they gave you your walking papers. I'm telling you they won't give you the time of day now. 'If you're not good enough for Communications, you're not good enough for Oil.' That'll be their attitude. You can bet on it."

Tidwell studied his drink in silence for a while, then took a hefty swallow.

"You're right, Clancy," he said softly. "But do you mind if I kid myself long enough to get good and drunk?"

"Sorry, Steve," apologized his friend. "It's just that for a minute there I thought you really believed what you were saying."

Tidwell lifted his glass in a mock toast.

"Well, here's to inferior superiors and inferior inferiors—the stuff armies are made of!"

He drained the glass and signaled for another.

"Really, Steve. You've got to admit the troops didn't let you down this time."

"True enough. But only because I gave them an assignment worthy of their talents: cannon fodder! 'Rush those machine guns and keep rushing until I say different!' Is it my imagination or is the quality of our troops actually getting worse? And speaking of that, who was that clown on guard with you?"

Clancy sighed.

"Maxwell. Would you believe he's one of our best?"

"That's what I mean! Ever since the corporations started building their own armies, all we get is superstars who can't follow orders and freeze up when they're shot at. Hell, give me some of the oldtimers like you and Hassan. If we could build our own force with the corporations' bankroll, if we could get our choice of the crop and pay them eighteen to forty grand a year, we could take over the world in a month."

"Then what would you do with it?"

"Hell, I don't know. I'm a soldier, not a politician. But damn it, I'm proud of my work and if nothing else, it offends my sense of aesthetics to see some of the slipshod methods and tactics that seem to abound in any war. So much could be done with just a few really good men."

"Well, we're supposed to be working with the best available men now. You should see the regular armies the governments field!"

"Regular armies! Wash your mouth out with Irish. And speaking of that. . . ."

The next round of drinks was arriving.

"Say Flo, love. Tell Bonnie I'm sorry if I was so short with her last round. If she comes by again, I'll try to make it up to her."

He made a casual pass at slipping his arm around her waist, but she sidestepped automatically without really noticing it.

"I'll tell her, Steve, but don't hold your breath about her coming back. I think you're safer when you're sulking!"

She turned to go and received a loud whack on her backside from Clancy. She squealed, then grinned, and did an exaggerated burlesque walk away while the two men roared with laughter.

"Well, at least it's good to see you're loosening up a little," commented Clancy as their laughter subsided. "For a while there, you had me worried."

"You know me. Pour enough Irish into me and I'll laugh through a holocaust! But you know, you're right, Clancy—about the men not letting me down, I mean. I think that's what's really irritating me about this whole thing."

He leaned back and rested his head against the wall.

"If the men had fallen down on the job, or if the plan had been faulty in its logic, or if I had tripped the fence beams, or any one of a dozen other possibilities, I could take it quite calmly. Hazards of the trade and all that. But to get canned over something that wasn't my fault really grates."

"They couldn't find any malfunction with the throat-mikes?"

"Just like the other two times. I personally supervised the technicians when they dismantled it, checked every part and connection, and nothing! Even I couldn't find anything wrong and believe me, I was looking hard. Take away the equipment failure excuse, and the only possibility is an unreliable commander, and Stevey boy gets his pink slip."

"Say, could you describe the internal circuitry of those things to me?"

In a flash the atmosphere changed. Tidwell was still leaning against the wall in a drunken pose, but his body was suddenly poised and his eyes were clear and wary.

"C'mon, Clancy. What is this? You know I can't breach confidence with an employer, even an ex-employer. If I did, I'd never work again."

Clancy sipped his drink unruffled by his friend's challenge.

"You know it, and I know it, but my fellow Oil Slickers don't know it. I just thought I'd toss the question out to make my pass legit. You know the routine. 'We're old buddies and he's just been canned. If you'll just give me a pass tonight I might be able to pour a few drinks into him and get him talking.' You know the bit."

"Well, you're at least partially successful." Tidwell hoisted his glass again, sipped, and set it down with a clink. "So much for frivolity! Do you have any winning ideas for my future?"

Clancy tasted his drink cautiously.

"I dunno, Steve. The last really big blow I was in

was the Russo-Chinese War."

"Well, how about that one? I know they shut
down their borders and went incommunicado after
it was over, but that's a big hunk of land and a lot of
people. There must be some skirmishes internally."

"I got out under the wire, but if you don't mind
working for another ideology, there might be something."

"Ideology, schmideology. Like I said before, I'm a
soldier, not a politician. Have you really got a line
of communication inside the Block?"

"Well. . . ."

"Excuse us, gentlemen."

The two mercenaries looked up to find a trio of
men standing at a short distance from their table.
One was Oriental, the other two Caucasian. All
were in business suits and carried attaché cases.

"If you would be so good as to join us in a private
room, I believe it would be to our mutual advantage."

"The pleasure is ours," replied Tidwell, formally
rising to follow. He caught Clancy's eye and raised
an eyebrow. Clancy winked back in agreement. This
had contract written all over it.

As they passed the bar, Flo flashed them an old
aviator's "thumbs-up" sign signifying that she had
noticed what was going on and their table would
still be waiting for them when they returned. To
further their hopes, the room they were led to was
one of the most expensive available at the bar—that
is, one the management guaranteed for its lack of
listening devices or interruptions. There were drinks
already waiting on the conference table, and the Oriental gestured for them to be seated.

"Allow me to introduce myself. I am Mr. Yamada."

His failure to introduce his companions identified them as bodyguards. Almost as a reflex, the two mercenaries swept them with a cold, appraising glance, then returned their attention to Yamada.

"Am I correct in assuming I am addressing Stephen Tidwell?" His eyes shifted. "Michael Clancy?"

The two men nodded silently. For the time being, they were content to let him do the talking.

"Am I further correct in my information that you have recently been dismissed by the Communications Combine, Mr. Tidwell?"

Again Steve nodded. Although he tried not to show it, inwardly he was irritated. What had they done? Gone through town posting notices?

Yamada reached into his pocket and withdrew two envelopes. Placing them on the table, he slid one to each of the two men.

"Each of these envelopes contains one thousand dollars, American. With them, I am purchasing your time for the duration of this conversation. Regardless of its outcome, I am relying on your professional integrity to keep the existence of this meeting as well as the content of the discussion itself in strictest confidence."

Again the two men nodded silently. This was the standard opening of a negotiating session, protecting both the mercenary and the person approaching him.

"Very well. Mr. Tidwell, we would like to contract your services for sixty thousand dollars a year plus benefits."

Clancy choked on his drink. Tidwell straightened in his chair.

"Sixty thousand. . . ."

"And Mr. Clancy, we would further like to contract your services for forty-five thousand dollars a year. This would of course not include the eighteen thousand five hundred dollars we would have to provide to enable you to terminate your contract with the Oil Coalition."

By this time, both men were gaping at him in undisguised astonishment. Clancy was the first to regain his composure.

"Mister, you don't beat around the bush, do you?"

"Excuse my asking," interrupted Steve, "but isn't that a rather large sum to offer without checking our records?"

"Believe me, Mr. Tidwell, we have checked your records. Both your records." Yamada smiled. "Let me assure you, gentlemen, this is not a casual offer. Rather, it is the climax of several months of exhaustive study and planning."

"Just what are we expected to do for this money?" asked Clancy cagily, sipping his drink without taking his eyes off the Oriental.

"You, Mr. Clancy, are to serve as aide and advisor to Mr. Tidwell. You, Mr. Tidwell, are to take command of the final training phases of, and lead into battle, a select force of men. You are to have final say as to qualifications of the troops as well as the tactics to be employed."

"Whose troops and in what battle are they to be employed?"

"I represent the Zaibatsu, a community of Japanese-based corporations, and the focus of our attention is the Oil vs. Communications war currently in process."

"You want us to lead troops against those idiots? Our pick of men and our tactics?" Clancy smiled. "Mister, you've got yourself a mercenary!"

Tidwell ignored his friend.

"I'd like a chance to view the force before I give you my final decision."

"Certainly, Mr. Tidwell," Yamada nodded. "We agree to this condition willingly because we are sure you will find the men at your disposal more than satisfactory."

"In that case, I think we are in agreement. Shall we start now?"

Tidwell started to rise, closely followed by Clancy, but Yamada waved them back into their seats.

"One last detail, gentlemen. Zaibatsu believes in complete honesty with its employees, and there is something I feel you should be aware of before accepting our offer. The difficulties you have been encountering recently, Mr. Tidwell, with your equipment and, Mr. Clancy, with your assignments, have been engineered by the Zaibatsu to weaken your ties with your current employers and insure your availability for our offer."

Again both men gaped at him.

"But . . . how?" blurted Tidwell finally.

"Mr. Clancy's commanding officer who showed such poor judgment in giving him his team assignments is in our employment and acting on our orders. And as for Mr. Tidwell's equipment failure. . . ." He turned a bland stare toward Steve. "Let us merely say that even though Communications holds the patent on the throat-mikes, the actual production was subcontracted to a Zaibatsu member. Something to do with the high cost of domestic labor. We took the liberty of making certain 'modifications' in their designs, all quite undetectable, with the result that we now have the capacity to cut off or override their command communications at will."

By this time the two mercenaries were beyond astonishment. Any anger they might have felt at being manipulated was swept away by the vast military implications of what they had just been told.

"You mean we can shut down their communications any time we want? And you have infiltrators at the command level of the Oiler forces?"

"In both forces, actually. Nor are those our only advantages. As I said earlier, this is not a casual effort. I trust you will be able to find some way to maximize the effect of our entry?"

With a forced calmness, Tidwell finished his drink, then rose and extended his hand across the table.

"Mr. Yamada, it's going to be a pleasure working for you!"

6

MAUSIER PAUSED TO WIPE THE BEADS OF sweat from his forehead, then bent to his task once more. Adjusting the high intensity lamp to a different angle, he picked up the watchmaker's tool and made a minute change in setting in the field terminal in front of him.

Without removing his eyepiece, he set aside the tool, reached over to the keyboard at the end of his workbench and input the data. Finally he leaned back and heaved a sigh. Done. He flexed his hands to restore circulation as he surveyed his handiwork.

The field terminal was a work of art. It could easily pass for a cigarette case, as it was supposed to. But if you pressed in three corners simultaneously, the inner metal lining folded out to reveal its interior workings, stark but functional. Two wires on mini-retracting reels were concealed in the hinge and could be pulled out to connect the unit to any phone. On the side of the lid was a tiny viewscreen. On the other side of the unit was a small keyboard containing both numbers and letters for data input. There was also the thumblock. Once the connection was made, the agent pressed his left thumb onto the metal square which would scan his print for comparison to the one on record in the master file. It would also check his body temperature to see if he was alive and his pulse to see if he was in an agitated state. If any of the three checks didn't match, the unit would self-destruct. Nothing as spectacular as an explosion—merely a small thermal unit to fuse the circuitry.

The Japanese had outdone themselves in producing these units for him. All he had to do was to make final adjustments for the individual's code number before it was issued. This allowed private communication with the individual client in addition to the general announcement postings.

Mausier smiled proudly at the unit. He had come a long way from his coincidental beginning in the business. At a cocktail party, one of his acquaintances had almost jokingly offered to pay him for details on a new machine modification Tom's company was working on. Tom had just as jokingly declined, but expressed an interest in the sincerity of the offer. The result had been an evening-long conversation in which his friend enlightened him as to the intricacies of corporate espionage and the high prices demanded and received due to the risks involved.

A short time after—within the week in fact—another friend of Tom's, this one within his own company, had admitted to him over coffee the dire financial straits he was in and how he was ready to take any reasonable risk to raise more money fast. Tom repeated his other friend's offer and volunteered to serve as a go-between.

In the years to follow, he served in a similar capacity for many similar transactions. Some of the people he dealt with were caught and dismissed for their activities, but he always escaped the repercussions due to the indirect nature of his involvement. Eventually, his clientele grew to the point to where he could quietly resign from the corporate world entirely and concentrate his efforts in this highly profitable venture.

Like most people who went into small businesses, the demands he made on himself were far in excess of any the corporation had ever made, yet he labored willingly and happily, realizing he was working because he wanted to and not because he had to. He was his own man, not the corporation's.

Mausier set aside the field terminal and stretched, rolling his shoulders slightly to ease the cramps from the prolonged tension of his work. It was late and he should go to bed. His wife was waiting patiently, probably reading. If he didn't go up soon, there would be hell to pay. As it was, she had already commented tersely several times in the last week about his lengthening his already long hours.

Finally he made up his mind. To hell with it! A few more minutes couldn't hurt. Having made his decision, he settled in at his desk and turned on his doodlescreen. It never crossed his mind that his wife might grow impatient enough to enter his office and interrupt his work. She might nag or scold or sulk once he entered the house, but she knew better than to interrupt him when he was working.

The workspace he keyed for was by now haunting-ly familiar. The Brazil workspace. He still thought of it as that even though by now it had spread to cover other areas. He should call it the Brazil-Iceland-Africa-Great Plains workspace, but the two items from Brazil had gotten him started, and it stayed in his mind as the Brazil workspace.

He concentrated on the screen. From the original two items, it had grown until the items listed covered over half the screen. Still, there were several things about the way the problem was progressing which perplexed him. A pattern was forming, but it wasn't making any sense.

He adjusted the controls on the screen and all the items blinked out except the names of the eight corporations. He leaned back and studied them. It was an unusual assortment of business concerns. There were four oil companies, a fishing concern, two mining corporations, and a communications conglomerate listed. What did they have in common? Some were international while some were local. Some were American in origin while some were based overseas. What was it they had in common?

Mausier frowned and played with the controls again. The eight names sorted themselves into pairs and moved apart, two to each corner of the screen. Now he had the two mining concerns (Africa), two of the oil corporations (the Great Plains), an oil corporation and the fishing concern (Iceland), and an oil corporation and the communications conglom-erate (Brazil) grouped together. It still didn't make

sense. It couldn't be mergers. The interests of the
Iceland pair and the Brazil pair were too dissimilar.
What's more, if the articles in the business journals
were to be believed, the mining interests in Africa
and the two oil concerns in the Great Plains were
bitter rivals. It couldn't be mergers. What was the
common factor of all eight corporations?

Almost unconsciously his hands twitched across
the controls and the notation "C-Block" appeared in
the center of the screen and blinked like a nagging
headache. Another pass over the controls and solid
lines appeared, linking each of the eight corporate
names with the C-Block notation.

The C-Block had identical standing offers in for
the same information on each of the eight corporations: *Any information on new hires and/or terminations at location.* Mausier's hands moved and
new lines grew like a spider web. One of the mining
concerns had identical standing orders in for the six
corporations at the other three locations, as did the
communications conglomerate. Both the oil concern and the fishing interest had identical requests
in for the pairs on the Great Plains and in Africa.

Mausier should have been very happy. With duplicate requests for the same information, he could
either collect his broker's percent for a double sale or
see his fee skyrocketed by a bidding war. He should
have been happy, but he wasn't. Whether or not the
corporations knew the C-Block was watching them,
they knew about each other and were watching each
other.

Watching each other for what? What was so vital
about the personnel at these locations? It was as
if there was a pool of specialized workers that the

corporations were passing back and forth, but what could it be? Engineers? They had new engineers beating down their doors with resumés. They could pick and choose at leisure. What was so special about the people at these locations? The geography and climate varied dramatically from location to location, so it wasn't a matter of acquiring a work force accustomed to working under a given set of conditions.

He suddenly realized he was working from negatives. Arriving at a solution by process of elimination was always tedious and often impossible due to the vast number of possibilities. It was always better to work with the facts at hand.

He cleared the screen and keyed for the other information requests coming from the eight corporations in question. He scanned them slowly and was again disappointed. Nothing out of the ordinary here. Just the usual interoffice political bickerings and ladder-climbing. How is a specific executive spending his time away from the office? Does anyone have any inside information on a rival's presentation plans? Any information on plans to shift a meeting site to another hotel? If interoffice communications ever improved, Mausier would lose a sizeable portion of his clientele. Still, there was nothing to add to his speculations.

He cleared the board again, this time using the display of a newspaper article. This was one of the few hard fact items in this file. He leaned forward to study it for the twentieth time.

His agent had not been lax or killed when he missed the rendezvous. He had been involved in a traffic accident and was still in the hospital. This article from a Brazilian newspaper gave the details of the incident. It all seemed very aboveboard. His agent had been stopped at a red light when another car hit him from behind, pushing him out into several lanes of busy cross-traffic. Nothing suspicious, except . . . except the driver of the car that hit him from behind was an employee of one of the corporations everyone was watching.

Mausier studied the article again, then shook his head. It had to be coincidence. He remembered what the rendezvous had been about, the sale of plans for some piece of electronics gear being used by the communications conglomerate. The driver, a Michael Clancy, was an employee of the Oil Combine. If he had been aware of the transaction, he would have either allowed it to happen or made some attempt to steal the information himself, which he hadn't done. It must be just what the article said it was—an accident while the employee was out joy riding with some waitress he had picked up in a bar.

Mausier suddenly realized he had been at the doodle-screen for nearly two hours. There would be hell to pay when he went home. Still, there was one more thing he wanted to check.

He cleared the article and keyed for one more item—today's entry to the file. There had been a new request on the board today from the C-Block, another request for personnel new hires and terminations. The group under study was a group of Japanese business concerns.

Mausier scowled at the request. It bothered him on several levels. First, it was a new factor in his already complicated puzzle, a new front, a new location. But there was something else that concerned him. One of the Japanese businesses listed was the company that manufactured his field terminals. For the first time, Mausier began to feel deep concern for the security of his scramblers.

7

"IT'S PETE, EDDIE. CAN I TALK WITH YOU FOR a few?"

"C'mon in, Pete. I've been expecting you."

The door slid open, and Pete stepped into Bush's office. The opti-print on the wall was blue today, matching Eddie's suit. Pete ignored it and sank into one of the numerous chairs dotting the office.

"Okay, boss, what went wrong?"

"With the meeting?"

"Yes, with the meeting. What happened?"

"You sound mad."

Pete blew a deep breath out, relaxing a little.

"A bit. More puzzled. I'm trying to be level-headed about all this but I get the feeling I'm not playing with all the cards."

"The meeting didn't go that badly. . . ."

"It didn't go that well either. And it isn't just

the meeting, it's the last couple weeks. All of a sudden you're dragging your feet on this thing. I just want to get the air clear between us and find out why."

Bush didn't answer immediately. Instead, he rose from his desk and keyed a cup of coffee from the Servo-Matic machine in the corner. Pete refrained from pointing out that there was already a steaming cup on the desk. He knew better than to crowd Eddie while he was collecting his thoughts.

"I guess you could say that I'm having second thoughts about our approach to this thing."

"The implementation or the basic idea?"

"Both. More the basic idea, though."

Pete closed his eyes and took a deep breath.

The team had been busting their butts on this thing, but it wouldn't go if Number One didn't believe in it.

"Okay, let's take it from the top. We all agree that if this thing blows up in our faces, we've got to have public support behind us. Right?"

"Right. And mass media is the fastest way to get it." Eddie's voice sounded mechanical.

"Now then, to do the job up front, to set the stage and create the atmosphere, we're proposing a saturation campaign of movies and specials, all on a military theme, stressing the right of the individual to protect his personal property and emphasizing the evils of government intervention."

"Whoa! Right there. Our whole strategy is based on the assumption that something will go wrong, that word will get out. At best, it comes off as negative thinking. At worst, it sounds like an open accusation of poor security or lack of employee loyalty. We aren't going to be able to sell this program if we come on hostile."

Pete tried to hide his impatience.

"That's why we slant the entire presentation on a 'better safe than sorry' format. C'mon, Eddie. We've been through all this before."

"And that government intervention thing. Why drag the government into it?"

"Okay, from the top. If this thing hits the news, our problem isn't going to be with the Oil Combine. There we've already got the white hats on. We're clear on everything we've done because all we've done is protect our own property. First, we sent the mercenaries in to protect our copper mines when the revolution threatened them; then we merely continued to defend the mines when Oil got the idea of using their mercenaries to take over the mines themselves. Everything we've done can be publicized as being for the good of the customer, us keeping costs down to keep prices down. Hell, even using our own mercenaries fits the pattern. We're paying for this out of our own pockets instead of using vital taxpayer dollars by lobbying for government troops. It was even our idea to rent land from Brazil to fight the war on instead of endangering the mines with on-site combat. As far as us against the Oil Combine, we've got nothing to worry about."

"I thought it was their idea to use Brazil for the fighting."

"It was, but we got it in writing first. That puts it in our pocket as far as history or the press is concerned. We've got 'em cold."

"That's well and good, but what's that got to do with government intervention?"

"If word of this thing gets out, the real battle is going to be with the government. You know Uncle Sammy—anything he can't tax he doesn't like, and anything he doesn't like he meddles with. It's within possibilities that he'll try to make us compromise with the Combine and divvy up the mines. If that happens, there will be a brawl, both in the courts and in Congress. If we're going to win that fight, we've got to have public support solidly behind us. That's where the saturation campaign comes in. If we can get the spark started before the specific case becomes public knowledge, it will be easy to fan it and point it in a direction. Hell, Eddie, you were the one who pointed it out in the first place."

"Well, I was just. . . ."

"You were just asking questions that we answered in the first week we had this assignment. Now I thought we had a pretty good working relationship going, Eddie. I could always count on you for a straight answer no matter how unpleasant it was. I'm asking you plain—what's going wrong? If you can't tell me, say so and I'll back off, but don't give me a smoke screen and pretend it's an answer!"

Bush was silent for a few moments, his eyes not meeting Pete's glare. Finally he sighed.

"You're right, Pete. I should have leveled with you sooner."

He opened a drawer on his desk and withdrew a sheath of papers, tossing them on the desk in front of Pete.

"Here, look at these."

Pete picked up the sheets and started leafing through them. They were photocopies of the rough drafts of some documents. Crossed-out paragraphs and note-filled margins abounded. Whatever they were, they were a long way from presentation state.

"What are they?"

"That's some of the rough drafts of Marcus's presentation."

Pete raised his eyebrows in inquiry.

"Don't ask how I got them. Let's just say they got detoured past a copier on their way to the shredder."

"Do you have stuff from Higgins too?"

Eddie made a disparaging gesture.

"Some, but not as much. He's pushing for a joint effort with the Oil people to save cost. Frankly, I don't think it has a snowball's chance in hell of being accepted. Marcus is the man I'm watching."

"Okay, what's he got here?"

"It all boils down to one assertion. He says we should win the war."

"Win the . . . really? Just like that?"

"Oh, there's lots of back-up. He works off the same supposition that we do—that if the war lasts long enough, the word will leak out. But instead of trying to cover up afterward, he wants to finish it before it leaks."

"Does the boy wonder bother to mention how we're supposed to do this?"

"Rather explicitly. We're supposed to outgun them."

"Hire more mercenaries? We've already. . . ."

"No, outgun them. Better equipment. So far everybody's been fighting with government surplus weapons modified for simulated combat. Anything really new the governments are keeping under top

security wraps. He's saying we should go directly
to the designers and manufacturers and outbid the
governments for the new stuff. That would give
us enough of an edge to finish the fight once and
for all."

"That'd cost us an arm and a leg!"

"Not as much as you'd think. He points out how
much the corporations pad any bill going to the government and suggests by exerting a little economic
pressure, we could drive the price down consider-
ably. Then again—pull page four out of that stack
for a minute."

"Got it."

"What you have there is a document he inter-
cepted. Apparently the bastard has inside information from the negotiating sessions."

Pete was scanning the page.

"What's a 'One-for-One Proposal'?"

"It's some new rule the Oil types are trying to
push through. Basically it means the mercenaries
would have to destroy equipment and ammunition
as if it had actually been used."

"That's insane!"

"Our negotiating team is giving it an eighty
percent probability of passing. If it does, cost
estimates for continuing the war go as high as
fifty thousand dollars a day."

Pete whistled appreciatively.

"With that tidbit under his arm, Marcus' proposal
doesn't sound nearly as expensive."

"So where does that leave us?"

Eddie pursed his lips.

"That's what's been bothering me. This proposed
program has a lot of sparkle and romance to it. It's

going to get a lot of support. If we decide to fight it, it's going to be an uphill battle."

A warning bell went off in the back of Pete's mind.

"Did you say 'if we decide. . . . '?"

Eddie sighed.

"There's one more bit of information that I haven't told you. It seems that Becker, Mr. Big himself, has been talking with Marcus at least once a week, sometimes daily. If he's taking a personal interest in seeing Marcus get ahead, we might want to think long and hard about our own careers before we set out to try to make the golden boy look bad."

8

THE CLIFF TOWERED GRIM AND FOREBODING,
fully the height of a three-story building. Except for
a few scrawny weeds dotting its face, indicating out-
croppings or crevasses, it was a sheer drop onto the
rockslide. It was enough of an obstacle that even
the strongest of heart would take time to look for
another route.

The man at the top of the cliff didn't look for
another route or even break stride as he sprinted
up to the edge of the precipice. He simply stepped
off the cliff into nothingness, as did the three men
following closely at his heels. For two long heartbeats they fell. By the second beat their swords were
drawn—the world-famous Katanas, samurai swords
unrivaled for centuries for their beauty, their crafts-
manship, and their razor edges. On the third heart-
beat they smashed into the rockslide, the impact

driving one man to his knees, forcing him to recover with a catlike forward roll. By the time he had regained his feet, the others were gone, darting and weaving through the straw dummies, swords flashing in the sun. He raced to join them, a flick of his sword decapitating the dummy nearest him.

The straw figures, twenty of them, were identical, save for a one-inch square of brightly colored cloth pinned to them, marking five red, five yellow, five white, and five green. As they moved, each man struck only at the dummies marked with his color, forcing them to learn target identification at a dead run. Some were marked in the center of the forehead, some in the small of the back. It was considered a cardinal sin to strike a target that was not yours. A man who did not identify his target before he struck could as easily kill friend as foe in a firefight.

The leader of the band dispatched his last target and returned his sword to its scabbard in a blur of motion as he turned. He sprinted back toward the cliff through the dummies, apparently oblivious to the deadly blades still flashing around him. The others followed him, sheathing their swords as they ran. The man who had fallen was lagging noticeably behind.

Scrambling up the rockslide, they threw themselves at the sheer cliff face and began climbing at a smooth effortless pace, finding handholds and toeholds where none could be seen. It was a long climb, and the distance between the men began to increase. Suddenly the second man in the formation dislodged a fist-sized rock that clattered down the cliffside. The third man rippled his body to one side and it missed him narrowly. The fourth man was not so lucky. The rock smashed into his right forearm and careened away. He lost his grip and dropped the fifteen feet back onto the rockslide.

He landed lightly in a three-point stance, straightened, and gazed ruefully at his arm. A jagged piece of bone protruded from the skin. Shaking his head slightly, he tucked the injured arm into the front of his uniform and began to climb again.

As he climbed, a small group of men appeared below him. They hurriedly cut down the remains of the straw dummies and began lashing new ones to the supporting poles. None of them looked up at the man struggling up the cliffside.

They had finished their job and disappeared by the time the lone man reached the top of the cliff. He did not pause or look back, but simply rolled to his feet and sprinted off again. As he did, five more men brushed past him, ignoring him completely, and flung themselves off the cliff.

Tidwell hit the hold button on the videotape machine and the figures froze in midair. He stared at the screen for several moments, then rose from his chair and paced slowly across the thick carpet of his apartment. Clancy was snoring softly on the sofa, half-buried in a sea of personnel folders. Tidwell ignored him and walked to the picture window where he stood and stared at the darkened training fields.

The door behind him opened and a young Japanese girl glided into the room. She was clad in traditional Japanese robes and was bearing a small tray of lacquered bamboo. She approached him softly and stood waiting until he noticed her presence.

"Thanks, Yamiko," he said, taking his fresh drink from her tray.

She gave a short bow and remained in place, looking at him. He tasted his drink, then realized she was still there.

"I'll be along shortly, love. There's just a few things I've got to think out."

He blew a kiss at her, and she giggled and retired from the room. As soon as she was gone, the smile dropped from his face like a mask. He slowly returned to his chair, leaned over, and hit the rewind button. When the desired point had been reached, he hit the slow motion button and stared at the screen.

The four figures floated softly to the earth. As they touched down, Tidwell leaned forward to watch their feet and legs. They were landing on uneven ground covered with rocks and small boulders, treacherous footing at best, but they handled it in stride. Their legs were spread and relaxed, moulding to the contour of their landing point; then those incredible thigh muscles bunched and flexed, acting like shock absorbers. Their rumps nearly touched the rocks before the momentum was halted, but halted it was.

Tidwell centered his attention on the man who was going to fall. His left foot touched down on a head-sized boulder that rolled away as his weight came to bear. He began to fall to his left, but twisted his torso back to the center line while deliberately buckling his right leg. Just as the awful physics of the situation seemed ready to smash him clumsily into the rocks, he tucked like a diver, curling around the glittering sword, and somersalted forward, rolling to his feet and continuing as if nothing had happened.

Tidwell shook his head in amazement. Less than a twentieth of a second. And he thought his reflexes were good.

The swordplay he had given up trying to follow. The blades seemed to have a life of their own, thirstily dragging the men from one target to the next. Then the leader turned. He twirled his sword in his left hand and stabbed the point toward his hip. An inch error in any direction would either lose the sword or run the owner through. It snaked into the scabbard like it had eyes.

Tidwell hit the hold button and stared at the figure on the screen. The face was that of an old Oriental, age drawing the skin tight across the face making it appear almost skull-like—Kumo. The old sensei who had been in command before Tidwell and Clancy were hired.

In the entire week they had been reviewing the troops, he had not seen Kumo show any kind of emotion. Not anger, not joy—nothing. But he was a demanding instructor and personally led the men in their training. The cliff was only the third station in a fifteen-station obstacle course Kumo had laid out. The troops ran the obstacle course every morning to loosen up for the rest of the day's training. To loosen up.

Tidwell advanced the tape to the sequence in which the man's arm was broken. As the incident unfolded, he recalled the balance of that episode. The man had finished the obstacle course, broken arm and all. But his speed suffered, and Kumo sent him back to run the course again *before* he reported to the infirmary to have his arm treated.

Yes, Kumo ran a rough school. No one could argue with his results, though. Tidwell had seen things in this last week that he had not previously believed physically possible.

Ejecting the tape cassette, he refiled it, selected another, and fed it into the viewer.

The man on the screen was the physical opposite of Kumo who knelt in the background. Where Kumo was thin to the point of looking frail, this man looked like you could hit him with a truck without doing significant damage. He was short, but wide and muscular, looking for all the world like a miniature fullback, complete with shoulder pads.

He stood blindfolded on a field of hard-packed earth. His pose was relaxed and serene. Suddenly another man appeared at the edge of the screen, sprinting forward with upraised sword. As he neared his stationary target, the sword flashed out in a horizontal cut aimed to decapitate the luck-less man. At the last instant before the sword struck, the blindfolded man ducked under the glittering blade and lashed out with a kick that took the running swordsman full in the stomach. The man dropped to the ground, doubled over in agony, as the blindfolded man resumed his original stance.

Another man crept onto the field, apparently try-ing to drag his fallen comrade back to the sidelines. When he reached the writhing figure, however, in-stead of attempting to assist him, the new man sprang over him high into the air, launching a fly-ing kick at the man with the blindfold. Again the blinded man countered, this time raising a forearm which caught the attacker's leg and flipped it in the air, dumping him on his head.

At this point, the swordsman, who apparently was not as injured as he had seemed, rolled over and aimed a vicious cut at the defender's legs. The blindfolded man took to the air, leaping over the sword, and drove a heel down into the swordsman's face. The man fell back and lay motionless, bleeding from both nostrils.

Without taking his eyes from the screen, Tidwell raised his voice.

"Hey, Clancy."

His friend sat up on the sofa, scattering folders onto the floor and blinking his eyes in disorientation.

"Yeah, Steve?"

"How do they do that?"

Clancy craned his neck around and peered at the screen. Three men were attacking simultaneously, one with an axe, two with their hands and feet. The blindfolded man parried, blocked, and countered, unruffled by death narrowly missing him at each turn.

"Oh, that's an old martial artist's drill—blindfold workouts. The theory is that if you lost one of your five senses, such as sight, the other four would be heightened to compensate. By working out blindfolded, you heighten the other senses without actually losing one."

"Have you done this drill before?"

Clancy shook his head. He was starting to come into focus again.

"Not personally. I've seen it done a couple of times, but nothing like this. These guys are good, and I mean really good."

"Who is that one, the powerhouse with the blind-fold?"

Clancy pawed through his folders.

"Here it is. His name's Aki. I won't read off all the black belts he holds; I can't pronounce half of them. He's one of the originals. One of the founding members of the martial arts cults that formed after that one author tried to get the army to return to the ancient ways, then killed himself when they laughed at him."

Tidwell shook his head.

"How many of the force came out of those cults?"

"About ninety-five percent. It's still incredible to me that the Zaibatsu had the foresight to start sponsoring those groups. That was over twenty years ago."

"Just goes to show what twenty years of training six days a week will do for you. Did you know some of the troops were raised into it by their parents? That they've been training in unarmed and armed combat since they could walk?"

"Yeah, I caught that. Incidentally, did I show you the results from the firing range today?"

"Spare me."

But Clancy was on his feet halfway to his case.

"They were firing Springfields today," he called back over his shoulder. "The old bolt-action jobs. Range at five hundred meters."

Tidwell sighed. These firing range reports were monotonous, but Clancy was a big firearms freak.

"Here we go. These are the worst ten." He waved a stack of photos at Tidwell. On each photo was a man-shaped silhouette target with a small irregularly shaped hole in the center of the chest.

"There isn't a single-shot grouping in there you couldn't cover with a nickel, and these are the worst."

"I assume they're still shooting five-shot groups." Clancy snorted.

"I don't think Kumo has let them hear of any other kind."

"Firing position?"

"Prone unsupported. Pencil scopes battlefield zeroed at four hundred meters."

Tidwell shook his head.

"I'll tell you, Clancy, man for man I've never seen anything like these guys. It's my studied and considered opinion that any one of them could take both of us one-handed. Even . . ."—he jerked a thumb at the figures on the screen behind them—" . . . even blindfolded."

On the screen, a man tried to stand at a distance and stab the blindfolded Aki with a spear, with disastrous results.

Clancy borrowed Tidwell's drink and took a sip.

"And you're still standing by your decision? About extending our entry date to the war by two months?"

"Now look, Clancy. . . ."

"I'm not arguing. Just checking."

"They aren't ready yet. They're still a pack of individuals. A highly trained mob is still a mob."

"What's Kumo's reaction? That's his established entry date you're extending."

"He was only thinking about the new 'super-weapons' when he set that date. He's been trained from birth to think of combat as an individual venture."

"Hey, those new weapons are really something, aren't they?"

"Superweapons or not, those men have to learn to function as a team before they'll be ready for the war. They said I would have free rein in choosing men and tactics, and by God, this time I'm not going into battle until they're ready. I don't care if it takes two months or two years."

"But Kumo. . . ."

"Kumo and I work for the same employer and they put *me* in charge. We'll move when *I* say we're ready."

Clancy shrugged his shoulders.

"Just asking, Steve. No need to . . . whoa. Could you back that up?"

He pointed excitedly at the screen. Tidwell obligingly hit the hold button. On the screen, two men were in the process of attacking simultaneously from both sides with swords. Images of Clancy and Tidwell were also on the screen standing on either side of Kumo.

"How far do you want it backed?"

"Back it up to where you interrupt the demonstration."

Tidwell obliged.

The scene began anew. There was an attacker on the screen cautiously circling Aki with a knife. Suddenly Tidwell appeared on the screen, closely followed by Clancy. Until this point they had been standing off-camera, watching the proceedings. Finally Tidwell could contain his feelings of skepticism no longer and stepped forward, silently holding his hand up to halt the action. He signaled the man with the knife to retire from the field, then turned and beckoned two specific men to approach him. With a series of quick flowing motions, he began to explain what he wanted.

"This is the part I want to see. Damn. You know, you're really good, Steve. You know how long it would take me to explain that using gestures? You'll have to coach me on it sometime. You used to fool around with the old Indian sign language a lot, didn't you? Steve?"

No reply came. Clancy tore his eyes away from the screen and shot a glance at Tidwell. Tidwell was sitting and staring at the screen. Every muscle in his body was suddenly tense—not rigid but poised, as if he was about to fight.

"What is it, Steve? Did you see something?"

Without answering, Tidwell stopped the film, reversed it, then started it again.

Again the knifeman circled. Again the two mercenaries appeared on the screen. Tidwell punched the hold button and the action froze.

He rose from his chair and slowly approached the screen. Then he thoughtfully sipped his drink and stared at a point away from the main action. He stared at Kumo. Kumo, the old sensei who never showed emotion. In the split second frozen by the camera, at the instant the two men stepped past him and interrupted the demonstration, in that fleeting moment as he looked at Tidwell's back, Kumo's face was contorted in an expression of raw, naked hatred.

9

FRED DISPENSED WITH THE WAITER'S PRO-
fuse thanks with an airy wave of his hand. He could
still vividly remember his high school days working
as a busboy, and as a result, habitually overtipped.

"Incredible! You feel it necessary to offer bribes
even for the simplest of services."

"Have you ever tried waiting on tables for twelve
hours solid, Ivan, old friend?"

"Yes. As a matter of fact, I have. My pay for the
entire twelve hours was less than you just gave that
man as a tip. But I did not mean to start another
argument, my friend. I was merely commenting on
the differences between how money is handled here
and how it was in my old homeland."

"Well, you're in America now."

"Yes, and as I said, I apologize. I meant no offense.

Please, for once let us end our meeting on a pleasant note."

"Fine by me."

Still maintaining an annoyed air, Fred rose to leave. However, he was puzzling over Ivan's last remark. Strange. It was the first time Ivan had ever apologized for getting under Fred's skin. If anything, he usually enjoyed doing it. In fact, Ivan had been acting strange all evening—no, make that all day.

Fred habitually spent more time studying his enemies than he did his friends, trying to memorize their quirks, their moods, anything that might give him an advantage in a confrontation. Quickly reviewing Ivan's reactions or lack thereof during the entire day, Fred would be willing to bet a month's wages that there was something bothering him. But what?

He paused for a moment to light a cigarette, and was rewarded by having Ivan rise to join him.

"Please, Fred. Might I walk with you for a bit?"

"Sure. I'm heading back to my hotel. Tag along and I'll buy you a drink. It's just across the park."

Ivan fell in step beside him and they left the restaurant in silence. Fred played the waiting game as they crossed the street and started down the sidewalk through the park. The night sounds of the city filtered through the air, giving a feeling of unreality, a persistent counterpoint to the deep shadows of the trees.

"Fred, we have been meeting privately at dinner for two months now. During these unofficial talks, I feel we have grown to know each other, yes?"

"I suppose."

C'mon, you bastard, spit it out. What's in the wind?

"I have a personal favor to ask of you."

Bingo! Deep in Fred's mind, a bright-eyed fox perked up its ears. If this was what it sounded like, he'd finally have his rival right where he wanted him. Nothing like having a member of the opposition over a barrel.

"What's the problem?"

"It is my daughter. I have recently received word she is alive . . . ah, I am getting ahead of myself. When I escaped . . . when I left my homeland, I was told that both my wife and daughter had been killed. Now word has been smuggled to me that my daughter is alive and living with friends. However, there is danger of the authorities finding her and I wish very badly to have her join me here in America."

"Have you told them at Oil?"

"Yes, but they cannot help me. They say I have not been working for them long enough."

"Bastards!"

"I have saved some money, but it is not enough. They say they can give me a loan in another six months, but I am afraid. My fellow workers will not help me. I am not well liked because of my many promotions. I thought that perhaps. . . ."

His voice trailed off into silence.

Fred's mind was racing. He'd help Ivan, of course. If Communications would not spring for the money, he'd do it out of his own pocket. This was too good an opportunity to miss. The big question was what could he get out of Ivan in return. Fred could probably shake him down for one big favor before Oil found out that their number two negotiator had sold out, but if he played it right, one would be plenty.

"Tell you what, Ivan. . . ."

"All right, you two! Hand 'em over!"

The two men spun to face the source of the interruption. A youth was standing on the sidewalk behind them; he must have either followed them or been waiting in the bushes. His voice was firm, but the gun in his hand wavered as he tried to cover the two men.

"C'mon! Give!"

The boy's voice cracked.

"Steady fella, we're giving."

Fred reached for his wallet, taking care to move slowly. If the kid had a knife he might have tried taking him, but he had a healthy respect for guns, particularly when they were held by nervous amateurs.

"No!"

All movement froze at the sound of Ivan's voice.

"What'd you say, Mister?"

"Ivan, for God's sake. . . ."

"I said, 'No!' "

He began to move toward the mugger.

"All my life I have been ordered around!"

"Stand back!"

"Ivan! Don't!"

Fred's mind was racing. He had to do something quickly.

"You have no right to. . . ."

The gun exploded in a flash of light, the report deafening in the night.

Ivan lurched backward. Shit! Fred threw his wallet at the mugger's face. The boy instinctively flinched away, raising his hands, and Fred was on him.

There was no style or finesse to Fred's attack. He snared the boy's gun hand with one ham-like fist, grabbed his shirt with the other, picked him up, and slammed him to the pavement. The boy arched and let out a muffled scream from the pain of impact. The scream was cut short as Fred hammered him into unconsciousness with two blows from his fist.

Breathing heavily, he pried the gun from the boy's fist, rose, retreated a few steps, then turned to look for Ivan. He was lying where he fell, unmoving, a large pool of blood oozing from beneath his loose-jointed form. Fred scrambled crab-wise over to look at him. His eyes were open and unseeing.

Shit! So close! So damn close!

For a moment, Fred was filled with an urge to stand up and kick the unconscious mugger.

You son-of-a-bitch! You've ruined everything!

He was still swearing to himself two and a half hours later when he left the police station. It had taken him almost half an hour to flag down a cop, a glowing testimonial to police efficiency. Now the body had been carted away, the mugger was safely locked up, and Fred was left with nothing.

Shit! Of all the bad breaks! Just when Ivan was about to bust open! Now he'd have to start from scratch with another negotiator. Well, maybe not from scratch. C'mon, Fred. Think. You're supposed to be able to make an advantage out of anything, even a disaster like this. Think!

He ignored the hail of a taxi driver and started the long walk back to his hotel. He covered near-ly eight blocks lost in thought, when suddenly an idea stopped him in his tracks. He stood there as he checked and rechecked the plan mentally, then looked around and ran back half a block to a pay phone.

He fumbled for some loose change, then fed a coin into the phone and hurriedly dialed a number.

"Mark? Fred here. I've got a hot assignment for you. . . . I don't give a damn. . . . Well, kick her ass out, this is important. . . . All right, I want you to get down to the police station and bail out the mugger that just killed Ivan. . . . That's right, Ivan Kramitz. . . . Yes, he's dead. . . . Look, I don't have time to explain now. Get down there and spring that mugger. I don't care how much it costs—spring him! And Mark, this time don't be too careful about covering your tracks. . . . That's right. I said don't be . . . right, let them know you work for Communications. . . . Look, I don't have time to explain now. Just do it."

He hung up the phone and sagged against the side of the phone booth. For several minutes he sat there, smiling. It was not a pretty smile.

"Before any business is transacted today, the negotiating team from Oil would like it read into the record that we are attending today's meeting under protest. We are both shocked and disappointed that Communications has insisted on convening today's meeting despite the death last night of one of our teammates. We only hope you will at least have the decency to keep today's business brief so that we might attend the funeral this afternoon."

A low growl of assent rose from the rest of the Oil team.

"We thank the First Negotiator of Oil for his comments. They will be duly noted in the records. The Chair now recognizes the Third Negotiator from Communications."

"Thank you, Mark." Fred rose to face the assemblage.

"May I assure you I will try to keep my proposal as brief as possible.

"Ivan's death last night was a serious blow to the Oil team. We share your grief and will miss him greatly. But, gentlemen, this should serve as another example of the hazards of war!"

There was a sudden stirring in the Oil team.

"Just as you pointed out in your one-for-one proposal that logistics is a real part of military strategy, so is assassination!"

"Are you trying to say you had Ivan killed?"

Fred smiled placidly at the interruptor.

"I have said no such thing. I merely point out that assassination of key personnel is as much or more a part of military tactics as moving boxes of ammo. Because of this, Communications proposes a conditional rider to your one-for-one proposal: that in a similar effort to insure realistic combat, all key personnel of both corporations be required to wear kill-suits at all times and be subject to the same rules of combat as the mercenaries. If we want realism, let's go for realism throughout. If not, we junk both ideas. Gentlemen, the time has come to put up or shut up!"

10

♈

THE MEN AND WOMEN OF THE FORCE WERE kneeling in the traditional student's position, backs straight, hands open, and palms resting down on their thighs. To all appearances they were at ease, listening to the morning's instruction.

This morning, however, the assembly was different. This morning, the raised instructor's platform held a dozen chairs filled by various corporation dignitaries. More importantly, the subject at hand was not instruction, but rather the formal transfer of command from Kumo to Tidwell.

Tidwell was both nervous and bored. He was bored because he was always bored by long speeches, particularly if he was one of the main subjects under discussion. Yet there was still the nervousness born from the anticipation of directly addressing the troops for the first time as their commander.

The speech was in English, as were all the speeches and instructions. One of the prerequisites for the force was a fluent knowledge of English. That didn't make it any the less boring.

He grimaced and looked about the platform again. The corporation officials were sitting in Tweedledee and Tweedledum similarity, blank-faced and attentive. If nothing else in this stint of duty, he was going to try to learn some of the Oriental inscrutability. Depending on the Oriental, they viewed Westerners with distaste or amusement because of the ease with which their emotions could be read in their expressions and actions. The keynote of the Orient was control, and it started with oneself.

Craning his neck slightly, he snuck a glance at Clancy, standing in an easy parade rest behind him. There was the Western equivalent to the Oriental inscrutability: the military man. Back straight, eyes straight ahead, face expressionless. Behind the mask, Clancy's mind would be as busy and opinionated as ever, but from viewing him, Tidwell did not have the faintest idea what he was thinking. In fact, Tidwell realized, he himself was currently the most animated figure on the platform. Suddenly self-conscious, he started to face front again when his eyes fell on Kumo.

Kumo was resplendent in his ceremonial robes. Protruding from his sash, at an unlikely angle to the Western eyes, was a samurai sword. Tidwell had heard that the sword had been in Kumo's family for over fifteen generations.

He held the weapon in almost a religious awe. Its history was longer than Tidwell's family tree, and it seemed to radiate a bloody aura of its own.

Anyone who didn't believe that a weapon absorbed something from the men who used it, from the men it killed, anyone who didn't believe that a weapon couldn't have an identity and personality of its own had never held a weapon with a past.

He suddenly snapped back into focus. The speaker was stepping away from the microphone, looking at him expectantly, as were the others on the platform. Apparently he had missed his introduction and was "on."

He rose slowly, using the delay to collect his scattered thoughts, and stepped to the edge of the platform, ignoring the microphone to address the force directly. A brief gust of wind rippled the uniforms of his audience, but aside from that, there was no movement or reaction.

"Traditionally, Japan has produced the finest fighting men in the world. The Samurai, the Ninjas, are all legendary for their prowess in battle."

There was no reaction from the force. Mentally he braced himself. Here we go!

"Also, traditionally, they have had the worst armies!"

The force stiffened without moving. Their faces remained immobile.

"The armies were unsuccessful because they fought as individuals, not as a team. As martial artists, you train the muscles of your body, the limbs of your body, to work together, to support each other. It would be unthinkable to attempt to fight if your arms and legs were allowed to move in uncontrolled random motions."

They were with him, grudgingly, seeing where his logic was going.

"Similarly, an army can only be effective if the men and women in it work in cooperation and coordination with each other."

He had made his point. Time to back off a little.

"Different cultures yield different fighting styles. I am not here to argue which style is better, for each style has its time and place. What must be decided is what style is necessary in which situation. In this case, that decision has been made by the executives of the Zaibatsu. As a result of that decision, I have been hired to train and lead you."

Now the crunch.

"You are about to enter a highly specialized war. To successfully fight in this war, you must abandon any ideas you may have of nationalism or glory. You are mercenaries, as I am a mercenary, in the employ of the Zaibatsu complex. As such, you must learn to fight, to think in a way which may be completely foreign to what you have learned in the past. To allow time for this training, the date for our entry into the war has been moved back by two months."

"I disagree, Mr. Tidwell."

The words were soft and quiet, but they carried to every corner of the assemblage. In an instant the air was electric. Kumo!

"I disagree with everything you have said."

There it was! The challenge! The gauntlet! Tidwell turned slowly to face his attacker. Kumo's words were polite and soft as a caress, but the act of interrupting, let alone disagreeing, carried as much emotional impact in the Orient as a Western drill sergeant screaming his head off.

"In combat, the action is too fast for conscious thought. If one had to pause and think about coordination of one's limbs, the battle would be lost before a decision was made. It is for this reason that martial artists train, so that each limb develops eyes of its own, a mind of its own. This enables a fighter to strike like lightning when an opening presents itself. Similarly, we train each man to be a self-contained unit, capable of making decisions and acting as the situation presents itself. This means he will never be hamstrung by slow decisions or a break in communications with his superior. As to your 'specialized war,' a trained fighting man should be able to adapt and function in any situation. Your failure to recognize this betrays your ignorance of warfare."

Tidwell shot a glance at the corporate officials. No one moved to interfere or defend. He was on his own. They were going to let the two of them settle it.

"Am I to understand that you are questioning the qualifications of Mr. Clancy and myself?" He tried to keep his voice as calm as Kumo's.

"There is nothing to question. After two weeks here, you presume to be an expert on our force and seek to change it. You expect the force to follow you because the corporation tells them to. This is childish. The only way one may lead fighting men is if he holds their respect. That respect must be earned. It cannot be ordered. So far, all we have for proof is words. If your knowledge of battle is so vastly superior to ours, perhaps you could demonstrate it by defeating one of the force that we might see with our own eyes you are fit to lead us."

Tidwell was thunderstruck. This was unheard of! In paperback novels, leaders would issue blanket challenges to their force to "any man who thinks he can lick me." In life it was never done. Leaders were chosen for their knowledge of strategy and tactics, not their individual fighting prowess. It was doubtful that either Patton or Rommel, or Genghis Khan for that matter, could beat any man in their command in a fistfight. No commander in his right mind would jeopardize his authority by entering into a brawl.

It crossed his mind to refuse the challenge. He had already acknowledged the superior ability of the Japanese in individual combat, contesting only their group tactics. Just as quickly he rejected the thought. No matter how insane it was, he could not refuse this challenge. He was in the Orient. To refuse would be to indicate cowardice, to lose face. He would have to fight this battle and win it.

"Sensei, I have publicly stated that the people of Japan have produced the greatest fighters in history. I will elaborate and say that I have no doubts that the men and women under your instruction equal or surpass those warriors of old in skill. Moreover, I must bow to your superior knowledge of their abilities and attitudes."

Kumo bowed his head slightly, acknowledging the compliment, but his eyes were still wary.

"However, what you tell me is that they must be convinced with action, not words. It has been always a characteristic of man that he can settle differences, pass his experiences from one generation to the next, and develop new ideas and concepts through the use of words. If you are correct in your appraisal of your students, if they are unable to be swayed by words, if the only way their respect can be earned is by action, then they are not men, they are animals."

Kumo's back stiffened.

"This is not surprising because you have trained them like animals."

There was an angry stirring in the ranks.

"Normally, I would stand aside for men and women of such training, for they could defeat me with ease. But you tell me they are animals. As such, I will accept your challenge, Kumo. I will stand and defeat the man or woman of your choice any time, any place, with any weapon, for I am a man, and a man does not fear an animal."

There were scattered angry cries from the ranks. First singly, then as a group, the force rose and stood at the ready position, wordlessly volunteering to champion the force by facing Tidwell.

The mercenary suppressed an impulse to smile at the sensei's predicament. Kumo had obviously planned to face Tidwell himself. In slanting his retort toward the force, Tidwell had successfully forced Kumo into choosing a member from the ranks. A teacher cannot defend his students without implying a lack of confidence in their prowess. If the abilities of a student are challenged, the student must answer the challenge. Terrific. Would you rather face a tiger or a gorilla?

"Mr. Tidwell, your answer is eloquent, if unwise. You are aware that such a contest would be fought to the death?"

Tidwell nodded. He hadn't been, but he was now. Inwardly, he gritted his teeth. Kumo wasn't leaving him any outs.

"Very well. The time will be now, the place here. For weapons, you may have your choice."

Clever bastard! He's waiting to see weapons choice before he picks my opponent.

"I'll fight as I stand."

"I will also allow you to choose your opponent. I have faith in each of my students."

Damn! He'd reversed it. Now if Tidwell didn't choose Kumo for an opponent, it would appear he was probing for a weaker foe.

Tidwell scanned the force slowly, while he pondered the problem. Finally he made his decision.

He turned to Kumo once more.

"I will face Aki."

There was a quiet murmur of surprise as Aki rose and approached the platform. Obviously Tidwell was not trying to pick a weak opponent.

The powerhouse bounded onto the platform and bowed to Kumo. Kumo addressed him in rapid Japanese, then much to everyone's astonishment, removed his sword and offered it to his student. Aki's glance flickered over Tidwell, then he gave a short bow, shaking his head in refusal. Raising his head in calm pride, he rattled off a quick statement in Japanese, then turned to face Tidwell. Kumo inclined his head, then returned the sword to his sash. He barked a few quick commands, and several men sprang to clear the platform, relocating the dignitaries and their chairs to positions in front of and facing the scene of the upcoming duel.

Tidwell shrugged out of his jacket and Clancy stepped forward to take it.

"Are you out of your bloody mind, Steve?" he murmured under his breath.

"Do you see any options?"

"You could have let me fight him. If Kumo can have a champion, you should be able to have one too."

"Thanks, but I'd rather handle this one myself. Nothing personal."

"Just remember the option next time, if there is a next time."

"C'mon Clancy, what could you do that I can't in a spot like this?"

"For openers, I could blow him away while he's bowing in."

Clancy opened his hand slightly to reveal the derringer he was palming. Tidwell recognized it at once as Clancy's favorite holdout weapon—two shots, loads exploding on impact, accurate to fifty feet in the hands of an expert, and Clancy was an expert.

"Tempting, but it wouldn't impress the troops much."

"But it would keep you alive!"

"Academic. We're committed now."

"Right. Win it!"

Win it. The mercenary's send-off. Tidwell focused his mind on that expression as he took his place facing Aki. At times like this when the chips were down, it meant a lot more than all the good lucks in the world.

Suddenly the solution to the problem occurred to him. Chancy, but worth a try!

"Clancy, give me a pad and pencil."

They appeared magically. No aide is complete without those tools. Tidwell scribbled something quickly on the top sheet, ripped it from the pad, and folded it twice.

"Give this to Mr. Yamada."

Clancy nodded and took the note, stashing the pad and pencil as he went.

Everything was ready now. With relatively few adaptations, a lecture assembly had been converted into an arena. As he was talking to Clancy, Tidwell had been testing the platform surface. It was smooth sanded wood, unvarnished and solid. He considered taking off his boots for better traction, but discarded the idea. He'd rather have the extra weight on his feet for the fight—increased impact and all that.

Kumo sat at the rear center of the platform, overseeing the proceedings as always. Then Clancy vaulted back onto the platform, his errand complete. Deliberately he strode across the platform and took a position beside Kumo on the side closest Tidwell. Kumo glared, but did not challenge the move.

Tidwell suppressed a smile. Score one for Clancy. This was not a class exercise and Kumo was not an impartial instructor. It was a duel, and the seconds were now in position. One thing was sure—if he ever took a contract to take on the devil, he wanted Clancy guarding his flanks.

But now there was work to be done. For the first time, he focused his attention on Aki, meeting his enemy's gaze directly. Aki was standing at the far end of the platform, relaxed and poised, eyes dead. The eyes showed neither fear nor anger. They simply watched, appraised, analyzed, and gave nothing in return. Tidwell realized that he was looking into a mirror, into the eyes of a killer. He realized it, accepted it, and put it out of his mind. He was ready.

He raised an eyebrow in question. Aki saw and gave a fractional nod of his head, more an acknowledgement than a bow, and the duel began.

Tidwell took one slow step forward and stopped, watching. Aki moved with leisurely grace into a wide, straddle-legged stance, and waited, watching.

Check! Aki was going to force Tidwell into making the opening move. He was putting his faith in his defense, in his ability to weather any attack Tidwell could throw at him and survive to finish the bout before his opponent could recover. However the duel went, it would be over quickly. Once Tidwell committed himself to an attack, it would either succeed or he would be dead.

Tidwell broke the tableau, moving diagonally to his right leisurely, almost sauntering. As he approached the edge of the platform he stopped, studied his opponent, then repeated the process, moving diagonally to the left. Aki stood unmoving, watching.

To an unschooled eye, it would appear almost as if Tidwell were an art connoisseur, viewing a statue from various angles. To the people watching, it was Aki's challenge. He was saying, "Pick your attack, pick your angle. I will stop you and kill you."

Finally Tidwell heaved a visible sigh. The decision was made. He moved slowly to the center of the platform, paused, considering Aki, then placed his hands behind his back and began moving toward him head-on. Theatrically he came, step by step, a study in slow motion. The question now was how close? How close would Aki let him come before launching a counterattack? Could he bait Aki into striking first? Committing first?

Ten feet separated them. Step. Seven feet. Step.

Tidwell's right fist flashed out, whipping wide for a back-knuckle strike to Aki's temple, a killing blow. In the same instant, Aki exploded into action, left arm coming up to block the strike, right fist driving out for a smashing punch to Tidwell's solar plexus. Then in midheartbeat, the pattern changed. Tidwell's left hand flashed out and the sun glinted off the blade of a stiletto lancing for the center of Aki's chest. Aki's counter-punch changed and his right arm snapped down to parry the knife-thrust.

Instead of catching Tidwell's forearm, the block came down on the raised knife point as the weapon was pivoted in midthrust to meet the counter. The point plunged into the forearm, hitting bone, and Tidwell ripped the arm open, drawing the knife back toward him. As his arm came back, Tidwell jerked his knee up, slamming it into the wounded arm, then straightened the leg, snapping the toe of his boot into the wound for a third hit as Aki jerked backward, splintering the bone and sending his opponent off balance. Aki reeled back in agony, then caught his balance and tried to take a good position, even though his right arm would no longer respond to his will. His eyes glinted hard now, a tiger at bay.

Tidwell bounded backward, away from his injured foe and backpedalled to the far end of the platform. As Aki moved to follow, he pegged the knife into the platform at his feet, dropped to one knee, and held his arms out from his body at shoulder height.

"Aki! Stop!"

Aki paused, puzzled.

"Stop and listen!"

Suspiciously, Aki retreated slowly to the far end of the platform, putting distance between himself and Tidwell, but he listened.

"Mr. Yamada! Will you read aloud the note I passed you before the fight began."

Mr. Yamada rose slowly from his seat with the other company officials, unfolded the note, and read:

"I will strike Aki's right forearm two to four times, then try to stop the fight."

He sat down and a murmur rippled through the force.

"The point of the fight was to determine if I was qualified to lead this force in battle. At this point I have shown that not only can I strike your champion repeatedly, but that I can predict his moves in advance. This will be my function as your commander, to guide you against an enemy I know and can predict, giving maximum effectiveness to your skills. Having demonstrated this ability, I wish to end this duel if my opponent agrees. I only hope he embraces the same philosophy I do—that if given a choice, I will not waste lives. I will not kill or sacrifice my men needlessly. That is the way of the martial arts, and the way of the mercenary. Aki! Do you agree with me that the duel is over?"

Their eyes met for a long moment. Then slowly Aki drew himself up and bowed.

Kumo sprang to his feet, his face livid. He barked an order at Aki. Still in the bow, Aki raised his head and looked at Kumo, then at Tidwell, then back at Kumo, and shook his head.

Clancy tensed, his hand going to his waistband. Tidwell caught his eyes and shook his head in a firm negative.

Kumo screamed a phrase in Japanese at Aki, then snatched the sword from his sash and started across the platform at Tidwell.

Tidwell watched coldly as the sensei took three steps toward him, then stood up. As he did, the leg he had been kneeling on flashed forward and kicked the knife like a placekicker going for an extra point. The point snapped off and the knife somersaulted forward, plunging hilt-deep into the chest of the charging swordsman. Kumo stopped, went to one knee, tried to rise, then the sword slipped from his grasp and he fell. For several minutes there was silence. Then Tidwell turned to address his force.

"A great man has died here today. Training is canceled for the rest of the day that we might honor his memory. Assembly will be at 0600 hours tomorrow to receive your new orders. Dismissed."

In silence, the force rose and began to disperse. Tidwell turned to view the body again. Aki was kneeling before his fallen sensei. In silence Tidwell picked up the sword, removed the scabbard from Kumo's sash and resheathed the weapon. He stared at the body for another moment, then turned and handed the sword to Aki. Their eyes met, then Tidwell bowed and turned away.

"Jesus Christ, Steve. Have you ever used that placekick stunt before? In combat?"

"Three times before. This is the second time it worked."

"I saw it but I still don't believe it. If I ever mouth off about your knives again, you can use one of them on me."

"Yeah, right. Say, can you be sure someone takes care of Aki's arm? I just want to go off and get drunk right now."

"Sure thing, Steve. Oh, someone wants to talk to you."

"Later, huh? I'm not up to it right now."

"It's the straw bosses."

Clancy jerked a thumb toward the row of company officials.

"Oh!"

Tidwell turned and started wearily toward the men because they were his employers and he was a mercenary.

11

"WILLARD?"

"Yeah, last night." Eddie Bush was visibly shaken as he lit a cigarette.

"I just got the call from Personnel. They got him in a movie theater."

"I'll tell the troops. Damn! You think they'll be more careful."

"I know what you mean. He wasn't even on the 'kill list'."

"No, I mean I thought *he'd* be more careful. On the 'kill list' or not, anyone who wears a kill-suit is fair game. They're asking for trouble, all of them. They shouldn't be surprised when it finds them."

"Hell, Pete. I wear a kill-suit. So does half the corporation staff now. It's a style, a fad, a status symbol."

"Well, I don't think that people are taking it seriously enough." Pete ground out his own cigarette viciously.

"Haven't we lost enough people already without playing games with the assassin teams?"

"Most of those were on the first day. It was kind of sudden, you know."

"The hell it was. There were memos and meetings going around for over a month. Did you ever get an accurate count of how many we lost the first day?"

"Seventeen, with six near misses. I guess nobody really stopped to think it through."

"That's what I mean about people not taking it seriously. Who came up with this crackpot scheme anyway?"

Bush made a face.

"As near as I can tell we did, but damned if I know why."

"There's some solid talk going around that it was an under-the-table agreement between the corporation hierarchies to weed out some of the management deadwood."

"The 'forced retirement' bit? Yeah, I've heard that, but I don't believe it. Corporations pull some pretty sleazy moves when it comes to personnel management, but I can't believe they'd sink that low. Three years on half-pay would really be rough. I'm not sure I could take it. Oh well, I suppose it could be worse. They could be using real bullets."

"That's happened, too," Pete retorted.

"It was in the rules at the start. After four shots with the quartz-beams, the assassin can use live ammo. If the players don't turn on their kill-suits, it's their own fault."

"Is yours turned on now?"

Eddie ran a hand inside his jacket to check the controls.

"It sure is."

"But you had to check to be sure."

"Yeah, I see what you mean."

"Besides, I wasn't talking about those kills. I was talking about the others. Did you hear what happened to Brumbolt?"

"Just a few rumors."

"They shot him down. With live ammo and real blood. You know why? Because he went to the theater the same night as a couple execs from his old department. They swear they didn't even know he was going to be there. In fact, they haven't even talked to him since he was 'killed' and went on half-pay, all according to the rules. The assassins who spotted him thought he was trying to pass some notes or something, and cut him down in the parking lot. That's the kind of real-kill I'm talking about."

Eddie pursed his lips in a silent whistle.

"I haven't heard about that. That's weird. It's like . . . like. . . ."

"Like we were in a war—that's what I've been trying to say. The big question is, what are we going to do about it?"

Eddie stiffened, his features hardening into a mask.

"Are we going to get into that again, Pete?"

"You're damn right we are. I mean, we are still on a team to submit recommendations, aren't we?"

"Only until we can be reassigned. The project is dead, Pete."

"But. . . ."

"But nothing! It's dead! Marcus has already submitted his recommendations and they've been accepted. The corporation has already sunk a hunk of money into the new weapons, and they won't be looking for new ways to raise costs."

"Eddie. . . ."

"So we are going to sit down and shut up because I don't want to make an ass of myself backing a set of recommendations that won't be followed."

"That's the part I don't buy. I think we'll be making bigger fools of ourselves if after spending all this time and money on our team, we don't come up with anything."

"But the cost. . . ."

"Cost, hell. If there's one thing I've learned in my years with this corporation, it's that there's always money to be had for a good idea."

"And if there's one thing you haven't learned, it's when to keep your mouth shut. If you had, then I'd be answering to you instead of you to me. In theory you're right, but we're dealing with reality, and like it or not, that's the way it is. Now I'm telling you to back down!"

The two men glared at each other for several moments; then Pete forced a deep breath.

"Tell you what, Eddie. I'll make you a deal—no, hear me out. I've got something in my car that I think will change your mind. If it doesn't, then I'll shut up and go along."

Eddie considered him for a moment.

"All right, bring it in. But I honestly can't think of anything you can come up with that will change my mind."

"You'll have to come with me. It's too bulky to bring in."

"Okay, anything to get this thing settled."

He rose, and the two men headed out into the executive corridor. Stepping onto the conveyor, they rode along in silence for several minutes. Finally Eddie cleared his throat.

"Sorry about blowing up in there, Pete. I guess I just don't understand why you're fighting this so hard. There'll be other assignments."

"For you maybe. Oh, turn here, I'm parked on the street. Rolled in a little late and the exec lot was full."

"Okay, but what was that you were saying?"

"Hmm? Oh! Just that I'm not sure how many more assignments will get thrown my way."

"Is that what's bothering you? Hell, don't worry. From what I can see in the meetings, a lot of the decision makers know who you are. That idea you had for using a dummy terrorist group to explain the shootings was a stroke of genius. It really saved our bacon when it came to dealing with the authorities."

"But it didn't go out with my name on it. Oh, out this door."

"Yeah. That was a bad deal. Well, it didn't go out with my name on it either. But don't worry. The people who count know it was your idea. You'll get other assignments. Say, where's your car?"

"Up the block a bit. Can you honestly say you think I'm going to get another assignment from a corporate vp?"

"Well, maybe not directly, but if I get one, you

can bet you'll be one of the cornerstones of the team. That much I can. . . ."

The bullet took him in the center of the chest. It was the first time Pete had seen the effects of one of the exploding bullets. Eddie Bush kind of blew up, pieces of his body splashing over the sidewalk. There was no doubt he was dead before he hit the pavement.

Pete waved a hand at the assassin on the roof across the street even though he couldn't see him, then stooped over the body. Moving quickly, he reached inside Eddie's jacket and switched the kill-suit controls to the "off" position. Then he stood and smiled down at the corpse.

Wha'dya know, another terrible accident. And Ed Bush wasn't even on the "kill list." Well, it was a risk he ran, wearing a kill-suit. It was only a matter of time before someone took him up on it. Terrible he had forgotten to turn his suit on.

Still smiling, he turned and ran back into the building to report the horrible incident.

12

MAUSIER SMILED AS HE READ THE LATEST information request on the board. Someone was trying to find out how their security was breached. A hefty sum was being offered as well as immunity from prosecution.

Obviously this client was not as knowledgeable in the field of industrial espionage as Mausier. He briefly considered not even posting the offer, but then decided to go ahead with it. His field agents needed a good laugh once in a while.

Mausier constantly daydreamed about secret agents crawling through the darkness, picking locks, climbing fences, bribing guards, and taking pictures in the dark with mini-cameras hidden in belt buckles. He daydreamed, but he knew it wasn't real. This client had apparently not learned to differentiate reality from daydreams. Agents didn't climb fences, they walked in through the main gate or the employment office—that is, if they walked in at all. A hefty number of his most successful clients were call girls or waitresses. Most of the information holders would be astounded to learn the grateful little girl they impressed with a one-hundred-dollar tip was actually making three times their annual salary.

Secretaries, janitors, and shipping/receiving clerks were all potential key agents, if they weren't already actively engaged in it. But the field was not limited to the "little people." Many of his clients were high-placed trusted executives who felt that seventy thousand dollars a year wasn't enough to make ends meet. Mausier didn't feel this was strange. In fact, his own years in the corporate world convinced him that many of the white-collar spies were driven to it because of the financial pressures of maintaining a social front equal to or better than their job rating. It was a source of vague amusement to him that many executives turned to industrial espionage to be able to afford to keep up with other executives who were already supplementing their incomes as spies.

There were still a few sneak thief spies in the business, but it was unlikely they would disclose their methods either. It would only mean they would have to work around tighter security on their next job.

His whining client was not likely to get an answer to his information request even though the corporate world was crawling with agents. Mausier smiled. In his opinion after years of watching the business, the most successful agents were auditors.

His smile faded as he turned to his doodlescreen. The project was becoming almost an obsession, claiming increasing portions of his time and concentration. The Brazil workspace was so full he could no longer display all items on the screen simultaneously. He thought he had the answer now, but so much of the pattern still didn't make sense.

The screen flickered and displayed a list of names. These were people employed by the nine corporations who had died recently. He sorted them by corporation, then chronologically. There was a pattern here. On one specific day there had been a surge of deaths in the two corporations listed for the Brazilian location. Within a matter of weeks it had spread to the other names on the list, with the exception of Japan. Japan was a misfit in many ways, but he put it out of his mind temporarily and focused on the others.

He tapped the keys, and a series of articles from newspapers and magazines began to display themselves on the screen. Each would show twice for thirty seconds—first the full article, then the portions Mausier had highlighted for summary display.

He watched them idly as they flashed past. He didn't buy the terrorist group story. In all his reading and study, he could not detect a similar increase in deaths in any corporation outside his list of nine— well, eight. He might have been willing to believe the theory of randomly picked target corporations had he not already been studying them as a unit. As it was, it was too pat to be a coincidence. His eight corporations were the only ones to be randomly picked by a mysterious terrorist group? Bullshit. This was a new development of something that had been going on before.

He interrupted the display to reference an information request from the U.S. government that had gone unanswered for more than a month. They were asking for any and all information about the terrorist group, and offering a price that was well beyond tempting. Nobody answered.

The closest anyone had come to catching a member was one nut with a bomb. Although he swore up and down he was a member of that mystical group, investigation discovered he was working alone with a bomb he had built in his basement. Even the newspapers conceded he was probably a loner who was trying to cash in on the international publicity generated by the hunt for the elusive assassins.

Nobody could get a solid lead no matter what price was offered. That was what gave Mausier his first clue. There was only one time before he had known of when all levels of information hunters, governmental and free lance, had come up empty-handed. That was the aftermath of the Russo-Chinese War, when the C-Block sealed itself up and began buying but never selling information. The only possible explanation was the terrorist group was a front manned by and covered for by the C-Block. After all, wasn't it their inquiries that initially alerted him to the tie-in between the nine—no, eight—corporations?

But there his logic fell apart. Why were they doing it? To infiltrate the corporate structure with their own people? If so, why did they request personnel listings? Wouldn't they know who they were sending in?

He put it out of his mind for the moment and keyed for another display. Japan. During the time period in question, there had only been one death in the Japanese companies under surveillance, and that was of old age.

An article from a martial arts magazine eulogized the passing of an old sensei who had retired from teaching to take over some obscure physical fitness program for Japanese industry. That couldn't possibly tie in with the other items—or could it?

Mausier wished for a moment that someone would put in a request for the coroner's report on the old man's death so he could see if it was actually available, but he shrugged it off as wishful thinking. It never occurred to him to request the information himself. That would be cheating! He'd work with the pieces as they were given to him.

Why had Japan escaped the notice of the assassins? In fact, from watching the information requests, they seemed to have escaped the notice of the other eight corporations. The only one requesting information on them was the C-Block. Were they unrelated to the puzzle, or were they in fact the people behind the assassins?

Mausier shook his head in bewilderment and keyed for another display. An article flashed on the screen. It was an account of the death of a corporate executive, Edward Bush, at the hands of one of the terrorist assassins. This held particular interest for Mausier, as Bush had been one of his clients.

According to the article, the incident had not been unlike a score of others. A long-range sniper working in broad daylight picked him off on the sidewalk in front of his office and escaped without a clue.

The pattern was so repetitious Mausier could almost sing it in his sleep.

He was willing to accept it as an unfortunate coincidence. Bush had been a buying, not a selling client, so it was unlikely that his death was linked in any way to his dealings with Mausier. Still, there was something afoot.

Bush's own corporation had submitted an information request for details surrounding his death. What made it strange was that they had not made any similar requests regarding any of their other executives killed by snipers. Bush had not been particularly high-ranked in the corporation. Why the sudden interest in his demise?

There was still another curious coincidence connected with Bush's death. The C-Block was also requesting details. They hadn't requested details on any of the corporate deaths until now. Clearly there was something strange about the killing, but what? Was it Bush or the manner of his death? If Mausier's theory about the C-Block team of assassins was correct, would they know all about the incident already? Maybe it was the Japanese after all. Those damn Japanese! Where did they fit into it all? Did they fit in at all?

Mausier suddenly became aware of sounds in the outer office and realized his employees were arriving. He hastily turned off his doodlescreen and began composing himself for the day's routine.

As he did, however, he made a mental note to himself. He was going to go out at noon. For years he had seesawed back and forth trying to weigh necessity against childish romanticizing, but now he had made up his mind. He was going to buy a gun. Whatever was going on, the game was being played for high stakes and he was sitting on too much information to ignore the potential danger in his position.

13

THE CLIFF WAS AS FOREBODING AS EVER; THE straw dummies waited passively at the base. Still, Tidwell realized his interest was at a peak as he sat waiting with Clancy for the next group to appear. The two mercenaries were perched on the lip of the cliff, dangling their legs idly, about five meters to the left of the trail.

They came, five of them darting silently from tree to tree like spirits. As they approached the cliff, the leader, a swarthy man in his thirties, held up his hand in a signal. The group froze, and he signaled one of the team forward. Tidwell smiled as a girl in her mid-twenties slung her rifle and dropped to her stomach, sliding forward to peer over the cliff. The leader knew damn well what was down there because he had run the course hundreds of times before, but he was playing it by the book and officially it was a new situation to be scouted.

The girl completed her survey, then slid backward for several meters before she rose to a half-crouch. Her hands flashed in a quick series of signals to the leader. Clancy nudged Tidwell, who smiled again, this time from flattered pleasure. Since he had taken over, the entire force had begun using his habit of sign language. It was a high compliment. The only trouble was that they had become proficient with it and had elaborated on his basic vocabulary to a point where he now sometimes had trouble following the signals as they flashed back and forth.

The leader made his decision. With a few abrupt gestures from him, the other three of the team, two men and a woman, slung their rifles and darted forward, diving full-speed off the cliff to confront their luckless "victims" below. The leader and the scout remained topside.

The two observing mercenaries straightened unconsciously. This was something new. The leader apparently had a new trick up his sleeve.

As his teammates sprinted forward, the leader reached over his shoulder and fished a coil of rope out of his pack. It was a black, lightweight silk line, with heavy knots tied in it every two feet for climbing. He located and grasped one end, tossing the coil to the scout. She caught it and flipped it over the cliff, while the leader secured his end around a small tree with a quick-release knot. This done, he faded back along the trail about ten meters to cover the rear, while the scout unslung her rifle and eased up to the edge of the cliff ready to cover her teammates below.

Clancy punched Tidwell's shoulder delightedly and flashed him a thumbs-up signal. Tidwell nodded in agreement. It was a sweet move. Now the three attackers below had an easy, secure route back out as well as cover fire if anything went wrong.

Tidwell felt like crowing. The reorganization of the force was working better than he would have dared hope. The whole thing had been a ridiculously simple three-step process. First, there had been a questionnaire asking eight questions: Which four people in the force would you most like to team with? Why? Who would you be least willing to team with? Why? Who would you be most willing to follow as a leader? Why? Who would you be least willing to follow as a leader? Why?

The next step was to pass the data through the computers a few times. Two jobs were done simultaneously: first, the five-man teams were established along the lines of preference stated by the individuals; second, the deadwood and misfits were weeded out to be sent back to other jobs in the corporate structure.

The final step was to pull various members of the teams for special accelerated training in the more specialized skills necessary in a fighting unit. He had had to argue with Clancy a little on this point, but had finally won. Clancy had felt the existing specialists should be seeded through the teams to round out the requirements regardless of preference lines, but Tidwell's inescapable logic was that in combat, you're better off with a mediocre machine gunner you trust and can work with than an expert machine gunner you wouldn't turn your back on.

From then on, the teams were inseparable. They bunked together, trained together, went on leave together; in short, they became a family. In fact,

several of the teams had formed along family lines
with mother, father, and offspring all on the same
team, though frequently the leadership went to one
of the offspring.

It was a weird, unorthodox way to organize an
army, but it was bearing fruit. The teams were tight-
knit and smooth running and highly prone to coming up with their own solutions to the tactical problems Tidwell was constantly inventing for them. It
was beyond a doubt the finest fighting force Tidwell
had ever been associated with.

The attackers were regaining the top of the cliff
now. Suddenly, a mischievous idea hit Tidwell. He
stood up and wigwagged the team leader. With a
few brief gestures he sketched out his orders. The
team leader nodded, and began signaling his team.
The scout recoiled the rope and tossed it to the
team leader. He caught it, stowed it in his pack,
surveyed the terrain, and faded back into a bush.
Tidwell checked the terrain and nodded to himself.
It was a good ambush. He couldn't see any of the
team even though he had seen four of them take
cover. He hadn't seen where the scout went after
she tossed the rope.

Clancy was smiling at him.

"Steve, you're a real son-of-a-bitch."

Tidwell shrugged modestly, and they settled back
to wait.

They didn't have to wait long. The next team
came into sight, jogging along the trail in a loose
group. The leader, a girl in her late teens that Clancy
was spending most of his off-hours with, spotted
the two sitting on the edge of the cliff. She smiled
and waved at them. They smiled and waved back

at her. They were still smiling when the ambush opened up.

The girl and the two men flanking her went down to the first burst of fire. The remaining two members dove smoothly under cover and started returning their fire.

Tidwell stood up.

"All right! Break it up!"

There was an abrupt cease-fire.

"Everybody over here!"

The two teams emerged from their hiding places and sprinted over to the two mercenaries. Tidwell tossed his "activator key" to one of the survivors of the second team who ducked off to "revive" his teammates.

"Okay. First off, ambushers. There's no point in laying an ambush if you're going to spring it too soon. Let 'em come all the way into the trap before you spring it. The way you did it, you're left with two survivors who've got you pinned down with your backs to a cliff!"

The "revived" members of the second team joined the group.

"Now then, victims! Those kill-suits are spoiling you rotten. You're supposed to be moving through disputed terrain. Don't bunch up where one burst can wipe out your whole team."

They were listening intently, soaking up everything he said.

"Okay, we've held up training enough. Report to the firing range after dinner for an extra hour's penalty tour."

The teams laughed as they resumed their training. Sending them to the firing range for a penalty tour was like sending a kid to Disneyland. Ever since the new weapons had arrived, the teams had to be driven away from the ranges. They even had to take head count at meals to be sure teams didn't skip eating to sneak out to the range for extra practice.

The girl leading the second team shot a black look at Clancy as she herded her team off the cliff.

"Now who's the son-of-a-bitch, Clancy old friend? Unless I miss my guess, she's going to have a few words for you tonight."

"Let her scream." Clancy's voice was chilly. "I'd rather see her gunned down here than when we're in live action. I wouldn't be doing her any favors to flash her warnings in training. Let her learn the hard way. Then she'll remember."

Tidwell smiled to himself. Underneath that easy-going nice guy exterior was as cold and hard-nosed a mercenary as he was. Maybe colder.

"Nit-picking aside, Clancy, what do you think?"

"Think? I'll tell you, Steve. I think they're the meanest, most versatile fighting force the world has ever seen, bar none. Like you say, we're nit-picking. They're as ready now as they're ever going to be."

Tidwell felt a tightening in his gut, but he kept it out of his voice.

"I'm glad our opinions concur, Clancy. I just received new orders from Yamada this morning. The jump-off date has been changed. We're moving out next week."

14

JUDY SIMMONS LANGUISHED PICTURESQUE-
ly in her chair, gazing deeply into the candle of their
now habitual table in the dimly lit restaurant. In
turn, Fred studied her cautiously as he sipped his
coffee. She was beyond a doubt one of the most
dangerous people he had ever encountered.

The two negotiators were enjoying their traditional meditative silence after dinner, a brief breathing
spell before they plunged back into the move and
countermove of bargaining over after-dinner drinks.

She was striking, the kind of beauty that turned
heads on the street. Yet hidden in that enticing
frame was a mind as sharp as a straight razor.

Fred had been frequently frustrated in his dealings
with Ivan. The man's stubbornness and steadfast
refusal to venture information beyond his instructions had been maddening at times. But his suc-
cessor, this lovely little armful, was a cat of a

different color. She would smile coyly and match him argument for argument, innuendo for innuendo, and mousetrap for mousetrap.

After four weeks, their talks were at a firm stalemate, neither showing any real advantage or handicap. The original swarm of jokes from his teammate about his "old man immune to the witch's charms" were slowly giving way to impatient proddings and mumbled accusations of his "deliberately prolonging the meetings." He was by no means immune to her mystique, but neither was he throwing the bout. The iron will and keen perception he had noted in the open meetings was even more prevalent when encountered head-on. No sir! She earned her victories, but she was lovely.

"Fred." The voice jarred him out of his reverie. "Can I talk to you about something? Apart from our usual dueling?"

Fred was mildly startled. Something was up. She was breaking pattern. Over his years of negotiating, he had become an unknowing expert on body language, and her whole being expressed a major change. Where she usually leaned back, maintaining personal distance, stretching occasionally, like a well-fed jungle cat, she was now leaning forward on her elbows, her whole body radiating a concentrated intensity. And her eyes—she was usually expressive. But now, her eyes were distant, either looking at the table in front of her or somewhere past his shoulder. It was almost as if she were embarrassed by what she was about to say. In the entire time he had covertly studied her at the meetings, and in the last four weeks of close personal contact, he had never seen her like this. Whatever was coming, it was coming from someplace besides her negotiator's instructions and guidelines.

"It's about the international currency thing that's come up. You were rather outspoken in the meeting today with your views against it."

"That's right. It's a half-baked idea. The costs for running a system like that would be astronomical. Why, just to safeguard against counterfeiting. . . ."

She interrupted with an annoyed wave of her hand as if she was shooing a bothersome fly.

"I know. I know. I heard you at the meeting today. You make nice speeches, but this time . . . this time I think you're barking up the wrong tree."

"Oh, bullshit! Just because your whiz kids came up with the idea doesn't mean. . . ."

"Will you listen to me! I don't like it either!"

Their eyes locked in angry glares. Silence reigned for a few moments before Fred registered what she had said and his anger gave way to embarrassment.

"Sorry. You didn't say anything at the meeting."

"I know. I couldn't believe it was really happening. It was like a nightmare and I kept waiting to wake up."

She stared at her coffee. Fred waited respectfully for her to regain her composure.

"Fred, you talk about the costs, but have you really thought it through? Have you really stopped to think about what would happen if the corporations got together and issued their own world-wide currency?"

She looked at him directly now, her dark eyes deep, almost pleading, as she continued.

"Money makes the world go 'round, and the governments issue the money. If we start issuing our own money, it might make international business a lot simpler and stabilize costs, but the government won't stand for it. They'll be all over us with everything they've got. And it won't be just one or two governments, it'll be all of them. Every single one of 'em united to tear the corporations down. I wouldn't be surprised if the C-Block didn't deal themselves in too. That's why I'm against it!"

Fred considered her words.

"Do you really think that would happen?"

"Do you see anything that would keep it from happening?"

Fred started to sip his coffee, then set it down again.

"All the nations . . . when . . . I'm going to have to think about that one."

He looked at her, and realized she was still staring into space.

"Hey! Judy!" His words were soft and concerned.

She looked at him and he realized her eyes were brimming with tears.

"Hey, this thing really has you scared, doesn't it?"

Instead of answering, she rose and fled to the ladies room.

Fred signaled for the check and pondered the situation. Well, he had always wondered what it would take to crack that controlled exterior. Now he knew.

The waiter swept by, leaving the small black tray with the tab on it in his wake.

Fred stared at it thoughtfully for a full minute, then dug out his wallet and carefully counted out a small stack of bills onto the tray. In a twinkling it disappeared with a small murmur of thanks from the waiter, and he lit a cigarette and settled down to wait.

A few minutes later, Judy appeared, face pale but her makeup intact or repaired.

"Sorry about that, Fred, but I. . . ."

"Shall we go now?" He rose casually, as if nothing had happened or been said.

"But what about the check?"

"I took care of it."

"Oh, Fred, it was my turn to pay."

"I took care of it."

"But it's going onto the expense account anyway. . . ."

"*I* took care of it."

She blinked at him in sudden realization.

"Oh."

"I'm taking you back to the hotel. You need a nightcap . . . somewhere where there aren't other people around."

15
♈

"SPARE CHANGE? HEY, MAN, ANY SPARE change?"

The youthful panhandlers were inevitable, even in a Brazilian airport. Tidwell strode on, ignoring the boy, but Clancy stopped and started digging in his pocket.

"Come on, Clancy! We've got to beat that mob through Customs."

"Yeah, ain't it a bitch?" the youth joined in. "Do you believe these gooks? It's been like this for almost a week."

Curiosity made Tidwell continue the conversation.

"Any word as to what they're doing?"

"Big tour program. Some Jap company is giving free tours instead of raises this year." He spat on the floor. "Damn cheap bastards. Haven't gotten a dime out of one of them yet."

"Here." Tidwell handed him a dollar. "This'll make up for some of it."

"Hey man, thanks. Say, take your bags to that skinny guy on the end and slip him ten, no hassle!"

The youth drifted off, looking for fresh game.

"Hypocrite!" accused Clancy under his breath. "Since when were you suddenly so generous."

"Since I could write it off on an expense account. That item is going in as a ten-dollar payment for an informant. C'mon, I'll buy you a drink out of the profits."

"Actually, I'd rather loiter around out here and make sure everything goes okay."

"Relax." Tidwell shot a glance down the terminal. "They're doing fine. Damndest invasion I've ever seen."

At the other end of the terminal, the rest of their infiltration group was gathered, taking pictures and chattering together excitedly. Clancy and Tidwell had arrived by commercial flight half an hour after the charter plane, but the group was still fluttering around getting organized. They were perfect, right down to the overloaded camera bags and the clipboards. Even with his practiced eye, Tidwell could not have distinguished his own crew of cold killers from a hundred other groups of Orientals which frequent the tourist routes of the world.

"Hey! There you are!"

Both men winced. The irritating voice of Harry Beckington was unmistakable. After seven hours of his company on the plane, the mercenaries had not even had to confer before dodging him as they got off the plane. He would have made nice camouflage, but. . . .

"Thought I lost you guys with all the slant-eyes in here!"

Their smiles were harder than usual to force.

"Sure are a lot of them," volunteered Clancy gamely.

"You know how they are—first a few, then you're hip-deep in 'em."

"That's the way it is, all right," smiled Tidwell.

"C'mon. Let me buy you boys a. . . ."

As he spoke, he gestured toward the bar, and collided with one of the "tour group." He collided with Aki.

There was no reason for Aki to be passing so close, except that there was no reason for him not to. He was returning from the souvenir stand and the group of three men happened to be in his path. One of the forces' instructions for the invasion was to not avoid each other. Nothing is as noticeable to a watchful eye as a group of people studiously ignoring each other. It would have been unnatural for Aki to alter his path, so he simply tried to walk past them, only to run into Beckington's wildly flailing arm.

Aki's arm was still in a sling from his duel with Tidwell, and it suffered the full brunt of the impact. He instinctively bounced back, and stumbled over Beckington's briefcase.

"Watch it, gook! Look what you did!"

Aki was the picture of politeness. He bobbed his head, smiling broadly.

"Please excuse. Most clumsy!"

"Excuse, hell. You're going to pick all that stuff up."

Beckington seized his injured arm angrily, pointing to the scattered papers on the floor.

"For Christsake, Beckington," interrupted Tidwell, "the man's got a bad arm."

"Injured, my ass. He's probably smuggling something. How 'bout it, gook? What are you smuggling?"

He shook the injured arm. Small beads of sweat appeared on Aki's forehead, but he kept smiling.

"No smuggle. Please—will pick up paper."

Beckington released him with a shove.

"Well, hurry up!"

"Careful, Beckington, he might know karate," cautioned Clancy.

"Shit! They don't scare me with that chop-chop crap!" snarled Beckington, but he stepped back anyway.

"Here are papers. Please excuse. Very clumsy."

Beckington gestured angrily. Aki set the papers down and retreated toward the other end of the terminal.

"Boy, that really frosts me. I mean, some people think just 'cause they're in another country they can get away with murder."

"Yeah, people like that really burn me, too," said Tidwell drily. The sarcasm was lost.

"Where were we? Oh yeah. I was going to buy you boys a drink. You ready?"

"Actually, we can't."

"Can't—why not?"

"Actually, we're with Alcoholics Anonymous. We're here to open a new branch," interrupted Clancy.

"Alcoholics Anonymous?"

"Yes," said Tidwell blandly. "On the national board, actually."

"But I thought you were drinking on the plane."

"Oh, that," interrupted Clancy. "Actually it was iced tea. We've found that lecturing people while we're traveling just alienates them, so we try to blend with the crowd until we have time to do some real work."

"Have you ever stopped to think what alcohol does to your nervous system? If you can hold on a second we've got some pamphlets here you could read."

Tidwell started rummaging energetically in his flight bag.

"Ah . . . actually I've got to run now. Nice talking with you boys."

He edged backward, started away toward the bar, then turned, smiled, and made a beeline for the men's room.

Tidwell collapsed in laughter.

"Alcoholics. . . . Oh Christ, Clancy, where do you come up with those from anyway?"

"Huh? Oh, just a quickie. It got rid of him, didn't it?"

"I'll say. Well, let's go before he comes back."

"Um, can we stall here for a few minutes, Steve?"

Tidwell stopped laughing in mid-breath.

"What is it? Trouble?"

"Nothing definite. Don't want to worry you if it's nothing. Just talk about something for a few minutes."

"Terrific. Remind me to fire you for insubordination. How about that Aki? Do you believe he managed to keep his cool through all that crap?"

"Uh-huh."

"That Beckington is a real shit. If we weren't under contract, I'd like nothing better than realigning his face a little."

"Uh-huh."

"Dammit, that's enough! If you don't tell me what's up, I'll cut your liquor allotment!"

"Well . . . we might have a little problem."

"C'mon, Clancy!"

"You saw where Beckington went?"

"Yeah, into the men's room. So?"

"So, Aki's in there."

"What?"

"Doubled back and ducked in while we were doing the A.A. bit with Beckington. Probably needed to take a painkiller."

"Who else is in there?"

"Just the two of them."

"Christ! You don't think Aki. . . ."

"Not out here in the open, but it must be awfully tempting in there."

The two men studied the ceiling in silence for several moments. Still no one emerged from the men's room. Finally Tidwell heaved a sigh and started for the door. Clancy held up a hand.

"C'mon Steve. Why not let him. . . ."

"Because we can't afford any attention. None at all. All we need is to have them detain all the Orientals in the airport for a police investigation. Now let's go!"

The mercenaries started for the door. Tidwell raised his hand to push his way in, and the door opened.

"Oh, hi boys. How's the 'dry' business? Just do me

a favor and don't close down the bars until after I've left the country, know what I mean?"

"Um . . . sure, Harry. Just for you."

"Well, see you around."

He brushed past them and strode toward the bar.

Almost mechanically, the two mercenaries pushed open the door and entered the washroom. Aki looked up inquiringly as he dried his hands on a blow-jet.

"Um . . . are you okay, Aki?"

"Certainly, Mr. Tidwell. Why do you ask?"

The two men shifted uncomfortably.

"We . . . ah . . . we just thought that after what happened outside. . . ."

Aki frowned for a moment, then suddenly smiled with realization.

"Ah! I see. You feared that I might. . . . Mr. Tidwell, I am a mercenary under contract. Rest assured I would do nothing to draw needless attention to our force or myself."

With that, the three mercenaries headed out into the terminal to continue the invasion.

16

♈

WOLFE! BIG BAD WOLFE! SO HE WAS FINALLY
going to talk to Wolfe.

Pete took the corner with an almost military precision. As usual, the executive corridor was empty.
Bad for one's image to be caught loitering in the
corridor. Without people, all efforts to make the
hall seem warm and friendly through the use of
pictures, hangings, or statues failed miserably. It
always looked like you were on your way to a fall-
out shelter or a secret underground military installation.

After three days, Wolfe had finally sent for him.
Well, Petey boy'd have a word or two for him.

He winced at his own false bravado. Who's kid-
ding whom, Pete? You're scared. No . . . not scared.
Nervous. Okay . . . admit it. Drag it out and let's
have a look at it.

Something's wrong. Very wrong. Not just that I didn't get the number one spot. Something else. After three weeks as acting head of the section, Wolfe shows up. Wolfe, of all people! Wolfe is notorious as a trouble-shooter and axeman here at the corporation. His stay in any job was usually brief and always bloody. So what? I've survived purges before. Yes, but he's been here three days and this will be my first time to see him alone. Usually a second in command works close with the new chief, shows him the ropes and points out the rough spots. Panic tactics. Yes . . . that's it. Let me sweat it out for three days, then the mysterious summons and I'll open up like a steamed clam, rat on everybody. That must be what he's doing. Well, it's working!

Okay! You've admitted it. Now take a deep breath and play it with a little style.

Right! Wolfe's door loomed before him. He took a deep breath, raised a knuckle, and tapped twice softly.

One . . . two . . . three heartbeats. Five. The light above the door flashed green. He turned the knob and entered.

Wolfe beamed at him as he rose from the desk. California casual and used car friendly.

"Come in, Hornsby. It's Pete, isn't it?"

"Yes, sir."

"That's Emil. Please, no formality."

They shook hands and Wolfe waved him into a chair.

"Sorry we haven't gotten together sooner, but we've got quite a problem here."

"That was obvious when they called you in." Pete smiled back at him.

"Oh?" Wolfe seemed both surprised and amused. "How so?"

"Well . . . you . . . that is, you have a bit of a reputation. . . ."

" . . . As an axeman?" Wolfe dismissed it with a wave of his hand.

"Quite exaggerated, I assure you. A bit annoying, actually. Makes people shy away from me."

"Oh, sorry I mentioned it."

"Quite the contrary, always glad to get a little feedback. Now, where were we?"

"The problem."

"Oh, yes! We have quite a problem. That problem, Pete, is you!"

"Me, sir?" Pete felt his hands starting to fidget.

"Yes. This is the second time you've been passed over for promotion, isn't it?"

"Well . . . yes . . . but I've been moving up. Slow and steady."

"Still, it's not a good sign."

"I've been pretty tied up on this war thing."

"It seems to indicate you aren't developing as fast as we hoped, or you hoped, for that matter," Wolfe continued as if he hadn't heard.

"But I haven't had a chance to get to know. . . ."

"So we've worked up a plan for your leaving. It involves six months on full pay and another. . . ."

"Now just a damn minute!" Pete was on his feet.

"Sit down, Peter. There's no need to shout."

"If you aren't happy with my performance, there *are* other alternatives, you know! I've been thinking of putting in for a transfer."

"Pete, I'm trying to be pleasant about. . . ."

"What about a transfer!"

"Look, Hornsby!" Wolfe's face was grim. "I've been trying to get you transferred! For a week before I came and for the last three days! Nobody wants you! Now sit down!"

Pete sank back into his chair.

"Now, as I was saying." Wolfe was again the pleasant salesman.

"Why?"

Wolfe pursed his lips for a long moment, then sighed and leaned back.

"Basically because of Eddie Bush."

"What about him?"

"Specifically the circumstances surrounding the way he died so conveniently for you."

"Now look! If you're trying to say. . . ."

"*If* we had any solid proof, Hornsby, we'd turn you over to the authorities and that would be that. As it stands, there are just suspicions, perhaps unfounded, but enough that no one wants you working under them. I don't want you, and no one else wants you."

Pete's eyes fell before his gaze.

"Now then, as I was saying, you'll get six months. . . ."

"How long do I have?"

"Beg your pardon?"

"You know what I mean."

Wolfe sighed. For the first time he looked sympathetic.

"There's an armed guard waiting in my reception area to escort you out. Your files and office are being placed under lock and key as we're talking now. If you come back Saturday, a guard will meet you at the gate and escort you to your office where he will watch while you have half an hour to remove your personal effects."

"Has my staff been told?"

"A memo was distributed as you entered my office."

Pete thought for several moments.

"Then there's nothing else to say, is there?"

"Well, you could let me tell you about the separation plan we've worked up for you. I think you'll find it more than fair."

"Save it. Send me a letter. Right now, I just want to leave."

"Very well."

Pete rose.

"You'll understand, sir, if I don't shake your hand?"

"Frankly," Wolfe's eyes were cold, "I hadn't planned to."

He strode through the common corridors, head high, ahead of his guard. He had a disembodied, unearthly feeling, like he was walking in a dream.

He was screwed! No one would hire him now. Job hunting at his pay level without a job or a recommendation!

C'mon, Pete! You can work it out later. First try to put a little style into the exit.

He forced himself back into focus and began to look around him. Maybe a few casual nods or a wink or a wave at a couple of people on his way out. He suddenly realized he didn't know anyone in the halls. Nobody looked at him. Not that they were avoiding his eyes; they were all busy and their eyes passed over him as unimportant. Just a few curious glances at the guard. He didn't see any of his staff.

Usually there were a few of them around.

The window! One of the office windows overlooked the executive parking lot! They would be watching from the window. Some to wave goodbye, some from morbid curiosity, but they'll be at the window! Okay, Petey boy. We'll show them bastards how Peter Hornsby goes to meet his fate.

He cleared the door, forcing a jaunty air into his walk. He found he couldn't whistle, but decided it didn't matter.

As he reached his car and fumbled for his keys, curiosity forced him to sneak one peek at the window.

No one was watching.

17

MAUSIER WINCED AS THE GUN UNDER HIS coat bumped against the edge of the viewscreen with a loud "klunk!" He shot a covert glance around the office, but no one else seemed to notice. He heaved a sigh of relief, but was promptly assailed with additional doubts. More likely the staff had noticed and known what had happened, but chose to ignore it. The fact he was now carrying a gun was common knowledge since the afternoon he had acidentally triggered the clamshell shoulder holster, and the weapon had slid from under his coat to bounce on the floor in front of the whole office. A few had raised their eyebrows in surprise, but the majority of them had merely smiled indulgently. Mausier had secretly writhed in agony under those smiles, as he was writhing now under their toler- ant silence. They obviously thought he was silly, a child with a toy gun pretending to be dangerous or endangered. They weren't aware of the potentially explosive and violent situation they were all living in.

Then again, how sure was he? Mausier considered for the hundredth time taking the gun back to the store. It was doing him no apparent good and causing him untold embarrassment. His wife never tired of making little digs about "that thing" when he stripped and cleaned it each night. Even though he weathered her taunts in stoic silence, it was beginning to take its toll on him.

He felt foolish. Who would want to attack him anyway? He wasn't a key figure; in fact, he wasn't a figure at all. He didn't make any decisions, he never even touched the various items of information his office posted and negotiated for. He was a watcher, not a doer. All he had was some wild guesses and theories based on information any number of people could have if they read extensively and thought about what they read. Why should anyone come after him specifically? More importantly, what could he do if they did?

The closest thing to an attack that had happened to him had occurred last week. He had been walking through the parking lot of a shopping center and a panel truck backed into him, knocking him sprawling. The driver could have backed over him as he lay on the pavement. Instead he stopped the truck and leaped out to help Mausier back to his feet, apologizing profusely and offering to buy him a drink. At the time, Mausier's gun was locked in the glove compartment of his car two hundred feet away. He had left it behind for fear of tripping the shoplifter detection devices in the store.

If it had been a real attempt on his life, he would be dead. What could he have done to stop it even if he had had the gun along? Shot the driver when he heard the gears engage? He could hurt a lot of innocent people that way. Besides, the modus operandi was wrong for the assassin teams. They preferred to work from long range with scoped rifles. Okay, if one of those had taken a shot at him, what would he do, assuming, of course, the assassin missed his first shot, which they didn't seem to do very often? Draw his handgun and try to outshoot him? A professional assassin two blocks away with a scoped rifle? Fat chance.

The handgun he carried was a Walther P-38, a nastily efficient, medium-sized automatic. Its double action allowed him to carry it with one round chambered and the hammer down and still have the ability to get off the first round by simply squeezing the trigger without fielding slides or anything. He practiced with it at a local firing range at least once a week until he considered himself a moderate shot. That is, he could put the entire clip into a man-sized target if it was close enough for him to hit it with a thrown rock.

He was comfortably content with his abilities, or had been until one afternoon when he noticed the young man practicing in the lane next to him was outshooting him easily, snapshooting from the hip. "Instinct shooting" the youth had called it, all the while bemoaning how much his abilities had atrophied since he left the service.

No, Mausier had long since abandoned any hopes he might have once entertained about outshooting

the pros. Still, he clung tenaciously to the weapon. It was a chance, a slim chance admittedly, but
still a chance. Without it, he would have no chance
at all.

He glanced at his watch. Another hour and the
workday would be over. He was anxious for the staff
to leave so he could return to his hobby. There were
two new items on the board today he was particularly eager to start digging on.

One was an information request from the oil corporation linked to the Brazilian branch of his pet
mystery. The request was so off-the-wall he almost
wondered if they were putting it on the board as a
confusion tactic. They wanted lists of any people
who had left service with the Treasury Department
of any country in the free world within the last year.
Special bonuses would be paid for leads on people
who had been directly involved with the minting of
currency.

Moneymakers? What in the world were they up
to? What possible mess could they have gotten
themselves into that would require money experts
above and beyond those already available to the
corporate world? Counterfeiting? If so, why didn't
they simply turn it over to the governments to
run down? Maybe the problem was so widespread
that they wanted to hush it up by handling it
themselves. Maybe it was so widespread they
were afraid of an economic panic if the truth
leaked out.

Mausier shook his head. He was groping at straws.
He'd have to hold off until he had time to scan the
files for additional details or related items. Instead,
he turned his thoughts to the other new item.

The C-Block had a new information request on the board. This one concerned the Japanese industries which they had been watching. They were asking for a complete listing of personnel taking the newly offered bonus world tour. If possible, they also wanted details as to timetables and rotation schedules.

Tour groups! His Brazilian workspace was getting overloaded with items. Soon he would either have to rent additional computer time or start weeding it down. Tour groups and moneymakers. This whole puzzle was starting to get out of hand.

Sometimes he wondered if he wasn't imagining it all. One of the hazards in the intelligence profession was getting hold of minor data and blowing it all out of proportion. If one tried hard enough, it was possible to take any three newspaper articles chosen at random and weave them into a conspiracy of national or international proportions.

Take as an example those items about the weapon-design corporations. Suddenly many of the corporations on his list were inquiring about who the arms designers were building what for. It had puzzled him for the longest time until he finally figured it out. They were exploring another possible lead on the assassin teams. If the teams were, in fact, using special weapons, someone was supplying them. Very clever, actually—an angle the governments hadn't thought of checking into yet. Now, if he were the overly suspicious and paranoid type, he could build those inquiries into . . . well, he didn't know what, but he could build it into something.

But tour groups? Where in the world did they tie into the picture? There was one thing which might be worth looking into. If he recalled the small article he had noticed on the Japanese tour correctly, their first stop on the world tour was Brazil. It was the first time he had been able to draw even the vaguest connection between the Japanese crew and the other groups of corporations on his list. It was shaky and probably purely coincidental, but it was still worth looking into.

His thoughts were interrupted by Ms. Witley, who told him a gentleman was in the lobby who wanted to talk to him about selling some information. Mausier was not enthused over the news and briefly considered stalling the visitor until the morning. Only occasionally did walk-ins have anything really worth selling, and they were always incredibly long-winded about the risks they had run to obtain their worthless bit of trivia. Still, there were occasional pieces of gold among the gravel, and he hadn't gotten where he was turning away potential clients.

With that in mind, he instructed Ms. Witley to fetch the man back to his office. When he arrived, Mausier's appraising eye quickly classified him as pure corporation. It was more than the distinctive conservative suit—it was the way he held himself. His shoulders were tense, his smile forced, and his jovial pleasantness almost painful. Definitely corporate, maybe middle management, obviously desperate, probably overestimating the value of his information.

"Nice little layout you've got here." The man took in the screens with a wave of his hand.

Mausier didn't smile. He was determined to keep this brief.

"Ms. Whitley said you had some information to sell?"

"Yes, I have some information on the terrorist assassin groups everybody's looking for."

Mausier was suddenly attentive.

"What kind of information?"

"Say, do you mind if I smoke?"

"I'd rather you didn't." Mausier nodded at the electronic gear lining the office.

"Thanks," said the man, lighting up. "Now where was I? Oh, yes. I guess I know more about the terrorists than anyone. You see, I'm the one who invented them for the corporations. . . ."

Mausier suddenly realized the man was more than slightly drunk. Still, he was intrigued by what he was saying.

"Excuse me, what did you say your name was again?"

"Hornsby, Peter Hornsby."

18

"TELL THE DRIVER TO SLOW UP. IT SHOULD be right along here somewhere."

"I still haven't seen the buses." Clancy scowled through the dust and bug-caked windshield of the truck.

"Don't worry, they'll be—there they are!"

The buses were rounding the curve ahead, bearing down on them with the leisurely pace characteristic of this country. Tidwell watched the vehicle occupants as they passed, craning his neck to see around the driver. The bus passengers smiled and waved joyously, but Tidwell noticed none of them took pictures.

The mercenaries smiled and waved back.

"The fix is in!" chortled Clancy.

"Did you see any empty seats?"

"One or two. Nothing noticeable."

"Good. Look, there it is up ahead."

Beside the road there was a small soft shoulder, one of the few along this hilly, jungled route. Without being told, the driver pulled off the road and stopped. They sat motionless for several long moments, then Aki stepped out of the brush and waved. At the signal, the driver cut the engine and got out of the car. The two mercenaries also piled out of the car, but unlike the driver, who leisurely began taking off his shirt, they strode around to the back of the truck and opened the twin doors. Two men were in the back, men of approximately the same description as and dressed identically to Tidwell and Clancy. They didn't say anything, but strode leisurely to the front of the truck and took the mercenaries' places in the cab. Like the driver, they had been briefed.

The two mercenaries turned their attention to the crates in the back. Aki joined them.

"Are the lookouts in place?"

"Yes, sir."

"You worry too much, Steve," chided Clancy. "We haven't seen another car on this road all day."

"I don't want this messed up by a bunch of gawking tourists."

"So we stop 'em. We've done it before and we've got the team to do it."

"And lose two hours covering up? No thanks."

"I'm going to check the teams. I'll send a couple back to give you a hand here."

He hopped out of the truck and strode down the road, entering the brush at the point where Aki had emerged.

Fifteen feet into the overgrowth was a clearing where the teams were undergoing their metamorphosis. Nine in the clearing, and one in the truck made ten. Two full teams, and the buses had looked full.

The team members were in various stages of dress and undress. One of the first things lost when the teams were formed was any vague vestige of modesty. The clothes had been cunningly designed and tailored. Linings were ripped from jackets and pants, false hems were removed, and the familiar kill-suits began to come into view.

Clancy arrived carrying the first case. He jerked his head and two already-clothed team members darted back toward the road. Setting the carton down, Clancy slit open the sealing tape with his pocket knife. He folded the flaps back, revealing a case of toy robots.

Easing them out onto the ground, he opened the false bottom where the swamp boots were kept. These were not new boots. They were the member's own broken-in boots. Clancy grabbed his pair and returned to a corner of the clearing to convert his clothes. One by one, the members claimed their boots and a robot and stooped to finish dressing.

Tidwell had worn his boots to speed the changing process. He whistled low and gestured, and a team member tossed him a robot. He caught it and opened the lid on its head in a practiced motion. Reaching in carefully, he removed the activator unit for his kill-suit and checked it carefully. Satisfied, he plugged it into his suit and rose to check the rest of the progress, resealing the lid on the robot and stacking it by the carton as he went.

Conversion was in full swing as more cartons arrived. The shoulder straps came off the camera gadget bags, separated, and were reinserted to form the backpacks. Fashionable belts with gaudy tooling were reversed to reveal a uniform black leather with accessory loops for weapons and ammunition.

Tidwell particularly wanted to check the weapons assembly. Packing material from the toy cartons was scooped into plastic bags, moistened down with a fluid from the bottles in the camera bags, and the resulting paste pressed into molds previously covered by the boots to form the rifle stocks. The camera tripods were dismounted, the telescoping legs separated for various purposes. First, the rounds of live ammo were emptied out and distributed. Tidwell smiled grimly at this. All the forces' weapons were 'convertibles'—that is, they were basically quartz-crystal weapons, but were also rigged to fire live ammo if the other forces tried to disclaim their entry into the war.

The larger section of the legs separated into three parts to form the barrels for both the flare pistols and the short double-barreled shotguns so deadly in close fighting. The middle sections were fitted with handles and a firing mechanism to serve as launchers for the mini-grenades which up to now had been carried in the thirty-five-millimeter film canisters hung from the pack straps. The smallest diameter section was used for the rifle barrel, fitted with a fountain pen telescopic sight. The firing mechanisms were cannibalized from the cameras and various toys which emerged and were reinserted in the cartons.

One carton only was not refilled with its original contents. This carton was filled with rubber daggers and swords—samurai swords. These were disbursed to the members, who used their fingernails to slice through and peel back the rubber coating to reveal the actual weapons, glittering and eager in the sun. These were not rigged for use on kill-suits.

The label on the empty box was pulled back to reveal another label declaring the contents camera parts, and the skeletons of the cannibalized cameras were loaded in, packed with the shreds of the outer clothing now torn to unrecognizable pieces.

The cartons were resealed and reloaded, and the truck was again sent along its way with a driver, two passengers, and a load of working toys and camera gear.

Tidwell watched it depart and smiled grimly. They were ready.

"Call in the lookouts, Clancy. We've got a long hike ahead of us."

"What's with Aki?"

The Oriental was running toward them waving excitedly.

"Sir! Mr. Yamada is on the radio."

"Yamada?"

"This could be trouble, Steve."

They returned hurriedly to the clearing where the team was gathered around the radio operator. Tidwell grabbed the mike.

"Tidwell here."

"Mr. Tidwell." Yamada's voice came through without static. "You are to proceed to the rendezvous point to meet with the other teams at all haste. Once there, do not, I repeat, do not carry out any action against the enemy until you have received further word from me."

Tidwell frowned, but kept his voice respectful.

"Message received. Might I ask why?"

"You are not to move against the enemy until we have determined who the enemy is."

"What the hell. . . ."

"Shut up, Clancy. Please clarify, Mr. Yamada."

"At the moment there is a cease-fire in effect on the war. The government of the United States has chosen to intervene."

19

CORPORATION WARS CHARGED

A federal grand jury was appointed today to investigate alleged involvement of several major corporations in open warfare with each other. The corporations have refused to comment on charges that they have been maintaining armies of mercenaries on their payrolls for the express purpose of waging war on each other. Included on the list of corporations charged were several major oil conglomerates as well as communications and fishing concerns. The repercussions may be international as some of the corporations involved (continued on p. 28)

CORPORATIONS DEFY ORDERS

In a joint press release issued this afternoon, the corporations under investigation for involvement in the alleged corporate wars flatly refused to comply with government directives to cease all hostilities toward each other of a

warlike nature and refrain from any future
activities. They openly challenge the government's authority to intervene in these conflicts,
pointing out that the wars are not currently
being conducted within the boundaries of the
U.S. or its territories. They have asked the
media to relay to the American people their
countercharges that the government is trying
to pressure them into submission by threat-
ening to move against the corporations' U.S.
holdings. They refer to those threats as "bla-
tant extortion" being carried on in the name
of justice, pointing out the widespread chaos
which would be caused if their services to the
nation were interrupted. (continued p. 18)

CORPORATE ASSASSIN TEAMS CHARGED

In the wake of yesterday's television broad-
casts in which the corporations explained the
'bloodless war' concept they claim they have
been practicing, new charges have been raised
that they have for some time been employing
teams of professional assassins to stalk rival
executives in the streets and offices of America.
Several instances were cited of actual deaths
incurred as a result of this practice, both among
the executives and innocent bystanders. While
not commenting on these charges, the corporations bitterly denied any connection with the
forceable abduction yesterday of state's witness
Peter Hornsby, whose information first brought
the corporate wars to the government's attention. There is still no clue in that abduction,
which left two U.S. Marshalls dead and (continued p. 6)

STRIKER PREDICTS WAR

Simon Striker, noted political analyst of the
long silent C-Block, has warned that if the new
armed might of the corporations is not checked

by the governments of the free world, it is highly probable that the C-Block will take direct action. "Such a threat could not be ignored by the party (continued p. 14)

ECONOMIST TO SPEAK TONIGHT

Dr. Kearns, Dean of the School of Economics at the Massachusetts Institute of Technology, will speak here tonight as part of his nationwide tour soliciting support for the controversial corporate actions recently discovered. It is Dr. Kearns' contention that the corporations' proposed international currency would bring much needed stability to the world's monetary situation. His talk will begin at 8:00 P.M. IN AUDITORIUM A OF THE ECONOMICS BUILDING. ADMISSION IS FREE TO THE PUBLIC.

AFRICANS JOIN CORPORATE OPPOSITION

The League of African Nations added their support to the rapidly growing list of countries seeking to control the multinational corporations. With the addition of these new allies, virtually all major nations of the free world are united in their opposition to the combined corporate powers. Plans are currently being formulated for a united armed intervention if the corporations continue to defy (continued p. 12)

WORLDWIDE PROTESTS SCHEDULED

Protest demonstrations are scheduled for noon tomorrow in every major city across the globe as citizen groups from all walks of life band together to voice their displeasure at the proposed governmental armed forces intervention in the corporate wars. War is perhaps the least popular endeavor governments embark on, and it is usually sold to the populace as a step necessary to ensure national security, a reason which many feel does not apply in this situation. Groups not usually prone to voicing protest have joined the movement, including several policemen's unions and civil servant organizations. Government officials (continued p. 8)

COURT MARTIALS THREATENED

Armed Forces officials announced today that any military personnel taking part in the planned demonstrations will be arrested and tried for taking part in a political rally, whether or not they are in uniform.

GOVERNMENT-CORPORATE TALKS SUSPENDED

Negotiation sessions seeking peaceful settlement between the combined corporations and the united free world governments came to an abrupt halt today when several government negotiators walked out of the sessions. Informed sources say that the eruption occurred as a result of an appeal on the part of the corporations to the governments to "call off a situation involving needless bloodshed which the government troops could not hope to win." It is believed that what they were aluding to were their alleged "superweapons" which the governments continue to discount. "A weapon is only as good as the man behind it," a high-ranked U.S. Army officer is quoted as saying. "And we have the best troops in the world." With scant hours remaining before the deadline (continued p. 7)

20

LIEUTENANT WORTHINGTON, U.S. ARMY, was relieved as the convoy pulled into the outskirts of town. He only wished his shoulders would relax. They were still tense to the point of aching. He tried to listen to the voices of the enlisted men riding in the back of the truck as they joked and sang, but shrugged it off in irritation.

The bloody fools. Didn't they know they had been in danger for the last hour? They were here to fight mercenaries, hardened professional killers. There had been at least a dozen places along the road through the jungle that seemed to be designed for an ambush, but the men chatted and laughed, seemingly oblivious to the fact the rifles on their laps were empty.

The lieutenant shook his head. That was one Army policy to which he took violent exception. He knew that only issuing ammunition when the troops were moving into a combat zone reduced accidents and fatal arguments, but dammit, for all intents and purposes, the whole country was a combat zone. It was fine and dandy to make policies when you were sitting safe and secure at the Pentagon desk looking at charts and statistics, but it wasn't reassuring when you were riding through potential ambush country with an empty weapon.

He shot a guilty sidelong glance at the driver. He wondered if the driver had noticed that Worthington had a live clip in his pistol. Probably not. He had smuggled it along and switched the clips in the john before they got on the trucks. Hell, even if he had noticed, he probably wouldn't report him. He was probably glad that someone in the truck had a loaded weapon along.

They were in town now. The soldiers in back were whooping and shouting crude comments at the women on the sidewalk. Worthington glanced out the window, idly studying the buildings as they rolled past. Suddenly he stiffened.

There, at a table of a sidewalk cafe, were two mercenaries in the now-famous kill-suits leisurely sipping drinks and chatting with two other men in civilian dress. The lieutenant reacted instantly.

"Stop the truck!"

"But sir. . . ."

"Stop the truck, dammit!"

Worthington was out of the truck even before it screeched to a halt, fumbling his pistol from its holster. He ignored the angry shouts behind him as the men in back were tossed about by the sudden braking action, and leveled his pistol at the mercenaries.

"Don't move, either of you!"

The men seemed not to hear him, continuing with their conversation.

"I said, Don't move!"

Still they ignored him. Worthington was starting to feel foolish, aware of the driver peering out the door behind him. He was about to repeat himself when one of the mercenaries noticed him. He tapped the other one on the arm, and the whole table craned their necks to look at the figure by the truck.

"You are to consider yourselves my prisoners. Put your hands on your head and face the wall!"

They listened to him, heads cocked in alert interest. When he was done, one of the mercenaries replied with a rude gesture of international significance. The others at the table rocked with laughter; then they returned to their conversation.

Worthington suddenly found himself ignored again. Reason vanished in a wave of anger and humiliation. Those bastards!

The gun barked and roared in his hand, startling him back to his senses. He had not intended to fire. His hand must have tightened nervously and. . . .

Wait a minute! Where were the mercenaries? He shot a nervous glance around. The table was deserted, but he could see the two men in civilian clothes lying on the floor covering their heads with their arms. Neither seemed to be injured. Thank God for that! There would have been hell to pay if he shot a civilian. But where were the mercenaries?

The men were starting to pile out of the truck behind him, clamoring to know what was going on. One thing was sure—he couldn't go hunting mercenaries with a platoon of men with empty rifles.

Suddenly a voice rang out from the far side of the street.

"Anybody hurt over there?"

"Clean miss!" rang out another voice from the darkened depths of the cafe.

The lieutenant squinted, but couldn't make out anyone.

"Are they wearing kill-suits?" came a third voice from farther down the street.

"As a matter of fact, they aren't!" shouted another voice from the alley alongside the cafe.

"That was live ammo?"

"I believe it was."

The men by the truck were milling about, craning their necks at the unseen voices. Worthington suddenly realized he was sweating.

"You hear that, boys? Live ammo!"

"Fine by us!"

The lieutenant opened his mouth to shout something, anything, but it was too late. His voice was drowned out by the first ragged barrage. He had time to register with horror that it was not even a solid hail of bullets that swept their convoy. It was a vicious barrage of snipers, masked marksmen. One bullet, one soldier. Then a grenade went off under the truck next to him and he stopped registering things.

There was no doubt in anyone's mind as to the unfortunate nature of the incident. For one thing, one of the men in civilian clothes sharing a drink with the mercenaries was an Italian officer with the Combined Government Troops who corroborated the corporations' claim the action was in response to an unprovoked attack by the convoy.

The fourth man was a civilian, a reporter with an

international news service. His syndicated account of the affair heaped more fuel on an already raging fire of protest on the home fronts against the troops, intervention in the corporate wars.

Even so, the corporations issued a formal note of apology to the government forces for the massacre. They further suggested that the government troops be more carefully instructed as to the niceties of off-hours behavior to avoid similar incidents in the future.

An angry flurry of memos did the rounds of the government forces trying vainly to find someone responsible for issuing the live ammo.

The mayor of the town was more direct and to the point. He withdrew the permission for the American troops to be quartered in the town, forcing them to bivouac outside the city limits. Further, he signed into law an ordinance forbidding the Americans from coming into town with any form of firearm, loaded or not, on their person.

This ordinance was rigidly enforced, and American soldiers in town were constantly subject to being stopped and searched by the local constable, to the delight of the mercenaries who frequently swaggered about with loaded firearms worn openly on their hips.

Had Lieutenant Worthington not been killed in the original incident, he would have doubtless been done in by his own men—if not by the troops under him, then definitely by his superiors.

The sniper raised his head a moment to check the scene below before settling in behind the sights of his rifle.

The layout was as it had been described to him.

The speaker stood at a microphone on a raised wooden platform in the square below him. The building behind him was a perfect backdrop. With the soft hollow-point bullets he was using, there would be no ricochets to endanger innocent bystanders in the small crowd which had assembled.

Again he lowered his head behind the scope and prepared for his shot. Suddenly, there was the sound of a "tunggg" and he felt the rifle vibrate slightly. He snapped his head upright and blinked in disbelief at what he saw. The barrel of his rifle was gone, sheared cleanly away by some unseen force.

He rolled over to look behind him and froze. Three men stood on the roof behind him. He hadn't heard them approach. Two were ordinary-looking, perhaps in better shape than the average person. The third was Oriental. It was the last man who commanded the sniper's attention. This was because of the long sword, bright in the sun, which the man was holding an inch in front of the sniper's throat.

The man behind the Oriental spoke.

"Hi guy! We've been expecting you."

The speaker was becoming redundant. The crowd was getting a little restless. Why did the man insist on repeating himself for the third and fourth time, not even bothering to change his phrasing much?

Suddenly there was a stir at the outer edge of the crowd. Four men were approaching the podium with a purposeful stride—well, three men shoving a fourth as they came. They bounded onto the platform, one taking over the microphone over the speaker's protests.

"Sorry, Senator, but part of the political tradition is allowing equal time to opposing points of view."

He turned to the crowd.

"Good afternoon, ladies and gentlemen. You've been very patient with the last speaker, so I'll try to keep this brief. I represent the corporations the Senator here has been attacking so vehemently."

The crowd stirred slightly, but remained in place, their curiosity piqued.

"Now, you may be impressed with the Senator's courage, attacking us so often publicly, as he has been doing lately, when it's known we have teams of assassins roaming the streets. We were impressed too. We were also a bit curious. It seemed to us he was almost inviting an assassination attempt. However, we ignored him, trusting the judgment of the general public to see him as the loudmouthed slanderer he is."

The Senator started forward angrily, but the man at the mike froze him with a glare.

"Then he changed. He switched from his pattern of half-truths and distortions that are a politician's stock in trade, and moved into the realm of outright lies. This worried us a bit. It occurred to us that if someone did take a shot at him, it would be blamed on us and give credence to all his lies. Because of this, we've been keeping a force of men on hand to guard him whenever he speaks to make sure nothing happens to him."

He paused and nodded to one of his colleagues. The man put his fingers in his mouth and whistled shrilly.

Immediately on the rooftops and in the windows of the buildings surrounding the square, groups of men and women stepped into view. They were all dressed in civilian clothes, but the timeliness of their appearance, as well as the uniform coldness with which they stared down at the crowd, left no doubt that they were all part of the same team.

The man whistled again, and the figures disappeared. The man at the mike continued.

"So we kept watching the Senator, and finally today we caught something. This gentleman has a rather interesting story to tell."

The sniper was suddenly thrust forward.

"What were you doing here today?"

"I want a lawyer. You can't. . . ."

The Oriental twitched. His fist was a blur as it flashed forward to strike the sniper's arm. The man screamed, but through it the crowd heard the bone break.

"What were you doing here today?" The questioner's voice was calm, as if nothing had happened.

"I. . . ."

"Louder!"

"I was supposed to shoot at the Senator."

"Were you supposed to hit him?"

"No." The man was swaying slightly from the pain in his arm.

"Who hired you?"

The man shook his head. The Oriental's fist lashed out again.

"The Senator!" The man screamed.

A murmur ran through the crowd. The Senator stepped hurriedly to the front of the platform.

"It's a lie!" he screamed. "They're trying to discredit me. They're faking it. That's one of their own men they're hitting. It's a fake."

The man with the microphone ignored him. Instead he pointed to a policeman in the crowd.

"Officer! There's usually a standing order about guarding political candidates. Why wasn't there anyone from the police watching those rooftops?"

The officer cupped his hands to shout back.

"The Senator insisted on minimum guards. He pulled rank on the Chief."

The crowd stared at the Senator, who shrank back before their gaze. The man with the mike continued.

"One of the Senator's claims is that the corporations would do away with free speech. I feel we have proved this afternoon that the statement is a lie. However, our businesses, like any businesses, depend on public support, and we will move to protect it. As you all know, there's a war on."

He turned to glare at the Senator.

"It is my personal opinion that we should make war on the warmakers. Our targets should be the people who send others out to fight. However, that is only my personal opinion. The only targets in my jurisdiction are front-line soldiers."

He looked out over the crowd again.

"Are there any reporters here? Good. When this man took money to discredit the corporations, he became a mercenary, the same as us. As such, he falls under the rules of the war. I would appreciate it if you would print this story as a warning to any other two-bit punks that think it would be a good idea to pose as a corporate mercenary."

He nodded to his colleagues on the platform. One of the men gave the sniper a violent shove that sent him sprawling off the platform, drew a pistol from under his jacket, and shot him.

The policeman was suspended for allowing the mercenaries to leave unchallenged, a suspension that caused a major walk-off on the police force.

The Senator was defeated in the next election.

The young Oriental couple ceased their conversation abruptly when they saw the group of soldiers, at least a dozen, on the sidewalk ahead of them. Without even consulting each other they crossed the street to avoid the potential trouble. Unfortunately, the soldiers had also spotted them and also crossed the street to block their progress. The couple turned to retrace their steps, but the soldiers, shouting now, ran to catch them.

Viewed up close, it was clear the men had been drinking. They pinned the couple in a half-circle, backing them against a wall, where the two politely inquired as to what the soldiers wanted. The soldiers admitted it was the lady who was the reason for their attention and invited her to accompany them as they continued on their spree. The lady politely declined, pointing out that she already had an escort. The soldiers waxed eloquent, pointing out the numerous and obvious shortcomings of the lady's escort, physically and probably financially. They allowed as how the fourteen of them would be better able to protect the lady from the numerous gentlemen of dubious intent she was bound to encounter on the street. Furthermore, they pointed out, even though their finances were admittedly depleted by their drinking, by pooling their money they could doubtless top any price her current escort had offered for her favors.

At this, her escort started forward to lodge a protest, but she laid a gentle restraining hand on his arm and stepped forward smiling. She pointed out that the soldiers were perhaps mistaken in several of their assumptions about the situation at hand. First, they were apparently under the impression that she was a call girl, when in truth she was gainfully employed by the corporate forces. Second, her escort for the evening was not a paying date, but rather her brother. Finally, she pointed out that while she thanked them for their concern and their offer, she was more than capable of taking care of herself, thank you.

By the time she was done explaining this last point, the soldiers had become rearranged. Their formation was no longer in a half-circle, but rather scattered loosely for several yards along the street. Also, their position in that formation was horizontal rather than vertical.

Her explanation complete, the lady took her brother's arm and they continued on their way. As they walked, one of the soldiers groaned and tried to rise. She drove the high heel of her shoe into his forehead without breaking stride.

Julian rolled down his window as the service station attendant came around to the side of his car.

"Fill it up with premium."

The attendant peered into the back seat of the car.

"Who do you work for, sir?"

"Salesman for a tool and die company."

"Got any company ID?"

"No, it's a small outfit. Could you fill it up—I'm in a hurry."

"Could you let me see a business card or your samples? If you're a salesman. . . ."

"All right, all right. I'll admit it. I work for the government. But. . . ."

The attendant's face froze into a mask.

"Sorry, sir." He started to turn away.

"Hey, wait a minute!" Julian sprang out of the car and hurried to catch up with the retreating figure. "C'mon, give me a break. I'm a crummy clerk. It's not like I had any say in the decisions."

"Sorry, sir, but. . . ."

"It's not like I'm on official business. I'm trying to get to my sister's wedding."

The attendant hesitated.

"Look, I'd like to help you, but if the home office found out we sold gas to a government employee, they'd pull our franchise."

"Nobody would have to know. Just look the other way for a few minutes and I'll pump it myself."

The man shook his head.

"Sorry, I can't risk it."

"I'll give you fifty dollars for half a tank. . . ."

But the attendant was gone.

Julian heaved a sigh and got back into his car. Once he left the station, though, his hangdog mask slipped away. Things were going well with the fuel boycott. It had been three weeks since he had had to report a station for breaking the rules. He checked his list for the location of the next station to check out.

The mercenary was wearing a jungle camouflage kill-suit. The hammock he was sprawled in was also jungle-camouflaged, as was the floppy brimmed hat currently obscuring his face as a sunscreen. He was snoring softly, seemingly oblivious to the insects buzzing around him.

"Hey Sarge!"

The slumbering figure didn't move.

"Hey Sarge!" the young private repeated without coming closer. Even though he was new, he wasn't dumb enough to try to wake the sleeping mercenary by shaking him.

"What is it, Turner?" His voice had the tolerant tone of one dealing with a whining child.

"The tank. You know, the one the detectors have been tracking for the last five hours? You said to wake you up if it got within five hundred meters. Well, it's here."

"Okay, you woke me up. Now let me go back to sleep. I'm still a little rocky from going into town last night."

The private fidgeted.

"But aren't we going to do anything?"

"Why should we? They'll never find us. Believe in your infrared screens, my son, believe."

He was starting to drift off to sleep again. The private persisted.

"But Sarge! I . . . uh . . . well, I thought we might . . . well, my performance review's coming up next week."

"Qualifying, huh? Well, don't worry. I'll give you my recommendation."

"I know, but I thought . . . well, you know how much more they notice your record if you've seen combat."

The sergeant sighed.

"All right. Is it rigged for quartz-beams?"

"The scanners say no."

"Is Betsy tracking it?"

"Seems to be. Shall I. . . ."

"Don't bother, I'll get it."

Without raising his hat to look, the sergeant

extended a leg off the hammock. The far end of his hammock was anchored on a complex mass of machinery, also covered with camouflaging. His questing toe found the firing button, which he prodded firmly. The machine hummed to life, and from its depths a beam darted out to be answered by the chill whump of an explosion in the distance.

The private was impressed.

"Wow, hey, thanks, Sarge."

"Don't mention it, kid."

"Say, uh, Sarge?"

"What is it, Turner?"

"Shouldn't we do something about the infantry support?"

"Are they coming this way?"

"No, it looks like they're headed back to camp, but shouldn't we. . . ."

"Look, kid." The Sergeant was drifting off again. "Lemme give you a little advice about those performance reviews. You don't want to load too much stuff onto 'em. The personnel folk might get the idea it's too easy."

This evening, the news on the corporate wars was the news itself. It seemed some underling at the FCC had appeared on a talk show and criticized the lack of impartiality shown by the media in their reporting on the corporate wars.

News commentators all across the globe pounced on this item as if they had never had anything to talk about before. They talked about freedom of speech. They talked about attempted governmental control of the media. They talked about how even public service corporations like the media were not safe from the clumsy iron fist of government intervention.

But one and all, they angrily defended their coverage of the corporate wars. The reason, they said, that there were so few reports viewing the government troop efforts in a favorable light was that there was little if anything favorable to be said for their unbroken record of failures. This was followed by a capsule summary of the wars since the governments stepped in. Some television channels did a half-hour special on the ineptitude of the government efforts. Some newspapers ran an entire supplement, some bitter, some sarcastic, but all pointing out the dismal incompetence displayed by the governments.

The man from the FCC was dismissed from his post.

The blood-warm waters of the Brazilian river were a welcome change from the deadly iciness of the Atlantic. The two frogmen, nearly invisible in their camouflaged wet kill-suits and bubbleless rebreather units, were extremely happy with the new loan labor program between the corporate mercenaries.

One of the men spotted a turtle and tapped the other's arm, gesturing for him to circle around and assist in its capture. His partner shook his head. This might have the trappings of a vacation, but they were still working. They were here on assignment and they had a job to do. The two men settled back in the weeds on the river bottom and waited.

It was oven hot in the armor-encased boat. The Greek officer in command mopped his brow and spoke in angry undertones to the men with him in the craft. It was hot, but this time there would be no mistakes. He peered out the gunslit at the passing shore as the boat whispered soundlessly upstream.

This time they had the bastards cold. He had the best men and the latest equipment on this mission, and a confirmed target to work with. This time it would be the laughing mercenaries who fell.

"Hello the boats?"

The men froze and looked at each other as the amplified voice echoed over the river.

"Yoo-hoo! We know you're in there."

The officer signaled frantically. One of his men took over the controls of the automount machine gun and peered into the periscope. The officer put his mouth near the gunslit, taking care to stand to one side of view.

"What do you want?"

"Before you guys start blasting away, you should know we have some people from the world press out here with us."

The officer clenched his fist in frustration. He shot a glance at his infrared sonar man who shrugged helplessly; there was no way he could sort out which blips were soldiers and which were reporters.

"We were just wondering," the voice continued "if you were willing to be captured or if we're going to have to kill you?"

The officer could see it all now. The lead on the target had been bait for a trap. The mercenaries were going to win again. Well, not this time. This boat had the latest armor and weaponry. They weren't going to surrender without a fight.

"You go to hell!" he screamed and shut the gunslit.

The mercenary on the shore turned to the reporters and shrugged.

"You'd better get your heads down."

With that, he triggered the remote control detonator switch on his control box, and the frogmen-planted charges removed the three boats from the scene.

The mercenary doubled over, gasping from the agony of his wounds. The dark African sky growled a response as lightning danced in the distance. He glanced up at it through a pink veil of pain. Damn Africa! He should have never agreed to this transfer.

He gripped his knife again and resumed his task. Moving with the exaggerated precision of a drunk, he cut another square of sod from the ground and set it neatly next to the others.

Stupid. Okay, so he had gotten lost. It happens. But damn it, it wasn't his kind of terrain. He sank the knife viciously into the ground and paused as a wave of pain washed over him from the sudden effort.

But walking into an enemy patrol. That was unforgivably careless, but he had been so relieved to hear voices.

He glanced at the sky again. He was running out of time. He picked up his rifle and started scraping up handfuls of dirt from the cleared area. Well, at least he got 'em. He was still one of the best in the world at close-in, fast pistol work, but there had been so many.

He sagged forward again as pain flooded his mind. He was wounded in at least four places in his chest cavity alone. Badly wounded. He hadn't looked to see how badly for fear he would simply give up and stop moving.

He eased himself forward until he was sitting in the shallow depression, legs straight in front of him. Laying his rifle beside him, he began lifting the pieces of sod and placing them on his feet and legs, forming a solid carpet again.

His head swam with pain. When he had gotten lost, his chances of survival had been low. Now they were zero.

But he had gotten them all. He clung to that as he worked, lying down now and covering his bloody chest.

And by God, they weren't going to have the satisfaction of finding his body. The coming rain would wash away his trail of blood and weld the sod together again. If they ever claimed a mercenary kill, it was going to be because they earned it and not because he had been stupid enough to get lost.

The rain was starting to fall as he lifted the last piece of sod in place over his face and shoulders.

21

TIDWELL TRUDGED THROUGH THE DARK-
ness trying to ignore the feeling of nakedness he had
without a rifle. He grinned to himself. This was a
wacky idea, but if it worked it would be beautiful.

"Okay, Steve, you're there!" Clancy's voice came
to him through his earplug. "If you take another
fifteen steps, you'll kick one."

He halted his forward progress, and covertly studied the underbrush as he fished out a cigarette. He
stalled a few more seconds fumbling for a match,
then grudgingly lit up. These guys are good. He
slowly exhaled a long plume of smoke.

"You can come out, gentlemen. All I want to do
is talk."

His voice seemed incredibly loud in the darkness,
even to him. He waited a few moments. The night
was still.

"Look, I don't have a white flag with me, so I'm pinpointing my position with a cigarette instead. I'd like to talk to your ranking officer or noncom."

There was still no response. If he didn't have absolute faith in his back-up, he would feel silly standing there talking to himself.

"I'd love to stand here all night, but the bugs are getting bad. Look, we know you're here. We've been tracking you through our scopes for over an hour now. If we wanted you dead, you'd be dead. If it will convince you, there are twenty of you and we know your positions. Now does that convince you or do I have to bounce a rock off a couple of you?"

He paused again. Suddenly, there was a soldier standing ten feet from him. He hadn't seen him stand up or step out of the bushes; it was as if he had sprung from the earth itself.

"It's about time. Want a smoke?"

"You wanted to talk, so talk."

The man sounded annoyed. Tidwell grinned to himself—probably upset that his crack team had been discovered.

"I've got a message for you. We're asking you once politely to withdraw your men."

"Give me one good reason why we should pull out, wise guy?"

"I can give you a list. First off, we found you. Right off the bat that should tell you your hotshots aren't as good as you'd like to think they are. Now, don't get me wrong, they're good—some of the best I've seen in a government force. But you're outclassed, friend. Our troops have been at this game since the time they could walk. Stack that up against your five years' service and you've got some idea where you stand in this war. A poor third in a two-sided fight!"

"That's your story."

"Let me spell it out for you. You're the advance scout of a company of light infantry that's bivouacked about fifteen miles back. They've been out here blundering around for over two weeks and I'm the first person you've seen to put your sights on. During that time, we've penetrated your defense at will, putting BANG signs on your ammo dump, green dye in your drinking water, Mickey Mouse Club badges on your tents while you're sleeping at night. The fact that you and your force aren't dead isn't because we've never had the chance."

"You're the guys who have been doing all that?"

"You want to know how many of us there are? Five, and two of us are women. A five-member team is all that it takes to keep a company of you bozos running in circles for half a month."

"So how come you haven't attacked?"

"Why? We don't want to fight you clowns. None of the corporation mercenaries do. We just want you to clear the hell out and leave us alone. Why are you out here anyway?"

"Well . . . supposedly we're trying to keep you from destroying the world economy."

"Bullshit. You wouldn't know a world economy if it bit you on the leg. Hell, man, the corporations have *been* the world economy for over half a century now."

"So you want us to pull back to camp?"

"No, we want you to pull out completely. The whole damn company—tell your CO we said so."

"And that's supposed to convince him?"

"No, but this might." Tidwell pulled a bulky envelope from inside his shirt and pitched it to the soldier who caught it deftly.

"What is it?"

"Well, you can't see them in this light, but it's a batch of pictures of your CO."

"And that's supposed to convince him?"

"They might. They were taken through a rifle scope. The cross hairs show up just swell."

"We'll show them to him. We were about to pull back anyway."

"Oh, just one more thing. If you could tell your men to leave their rifles behind when they go."

"What!"

"You can come back tomorrow and pick them up, but we want to be sure you pass the message to your CO, and showing up without your rifles will make sure you don't forget to talk to him."

"Tell you what, fella. Why don't you come along and tell him personally. We're supposed to be looking for prisoners to interrogate and I guess you'll do just fine!"

"You know, I get the distinct impression you think I'm bluffing. Very well; which impresses you more—distance work or close quarters?"

"What?"

"Never mind, we'll give you a quick demo of each. Um, tell your men to ease off their triggers. There's going to be some noise, quite harmless of course, but I wouldn't want to see you all get wiped out because someone flinched off a shot."

"What are you talking. . . ."

The night was rent by two ear-splitting explosions, one to their left, one to their right. Two full heartbeats behind the blast came the unmistakable twin flat cracks of the rifle reports.

"In case you're wondering, those shots were squeezed off by my partner—the one I was telling you about who is two miles back. He's firing the mercury-tipped bullets you've heard about. Nasty things. Blow a man open like a ripe melon."

"Jesus Christ!"

"But you're a sneaky-pete type, so you'll probably be more impressed by night movement. Hang onto yourself, sonny."

A shotgun blast went off into the air half-way between the two men, and one of Tidwell's teammates sat up from where he had been lying prone in the calf-high undergrowth.

"Now then, little man." Tidwell's voice was hard. "Let's not hear any more crap about taking prisoners. I suggest you take your underpaid boy scouts and get the hell out of our jungle before we start playing rough."

Tidwell was in the blackout tent scanning the radio transcripts when Clancy burst through the double-flap entrance.

"Worked like a charm. They didn't stop until they got back to their camp. If they didn't wet their pants when that shotgun went off, it's only 'cause they haven't had anything to drink for twenty-four hours."

"Speaking of drinks, help yourself."

"Thanks," beamed Clancy, pouring himself a dollop of Irish. "What a crazy way to fight a war. I wonder who came up with this idea?"

" 'The object of war is not to destroy the enemy, but rather to destroy his will to resist.' Von Clausewitz, *On War*. The idea goes way back, Clancy. We're just carrying it out to the nth degree. Have you seen the latest?"

"What? The bit about our robot planes dropping sacks of flour on the steps of the White House?"

"No, the release about the high-altitude reconnaissance planes."

"What's the gist of it?"

"Basically the corporations sent a memo to the governments and the press citing the exact times high-altitude reconnaissance planes had flown over the zone in the last week. They pointed out that we were tracking them easily while our own troops were protected from the infrared snoop by jamming screens, and would they kindly refrain from sending them out or we would be forced to start downing them to eliminate the nuisance."

"Can we do it?"

"I don't think our force has anything that could, but that doesn't mean *someone* on the corporate team doesn't have a gimmick. Remember last month when the governments called a corporate bluff and we blew up one of their destroyers offshore?"

"Yeah. You know, that kind of gets me down, though—all the gimmick warfare. It takes the personal touch out of things."

"How about the 'gunsight' photos? You can't get much more personal than that. I bet a lot of governmental big mouths changed their tune when they saw themselves in the cross hairs."

"Tell me honestly, Steve—do you think we're going to win?"

"I don't see how it can go any other way. There's no way they can catch us short of saturation bombing or nukes, and public opinion is too much against them.

Hell, they're having a hard time with the pressures folks are putting on over this united effort. A third of the governments have already had to pull their troops. It's only a matter of time before the rest of them have to bail out."

"What then?"

"What do you mean?"

"Just that. Okay, the governments pull their troops out, effectively admitting they don't have the military power to police the corporations. What then?"

22

THE CROWDS OF CURIOSITY SEEKERS THREAT-
ened to choke off the street and probably would
have if not physically restrained by the lines of armed
government troops holding them at bay in the shadow of the poshest hotel in Rio de Janeiro. Even so,
a sizeable crowd gathered around the limousines
as they drew to a halt at the curb and had to be
cleared back by the bodyguards who emerged from
the autos first.

This smaller mob were members of the press who
passed unhindered through the lines of troops with
a wave of a media card. The troops were under strict
orders not to affront the press, who had been adding
volume to the already thunderous chorus of public
protest against the governments' actions. Even the
papers who had earlier supported the governments
were now scathingly critical of the armed forces'

ineffectiveness and inability to deal with the corporations. The governments did not need any more bad press.

Three men emerged from the limousines and headed for the door of the hotel. At their appearance, the reporters surged forward again and the men stopped, apparently consenting to giving a brief statement.

Several stories up, in a window of the hotel across the street from the activity, a machine was tracking the movements of the three men. Deeper in the room, well out of sight of the window, a small group of uniformed technicians were feverishly processing the data being collected by the combination closed-circuit television–shotgun mike. Their work was being closely supervised by a nervous officer.

"Are you sure, Corporal?"

"Positive, sir. Identification is confirmed on all three targets. A/V tapes and voice prints all match."

The officer squinted at the three figures in the monitor screen.

"Becker for Communications, Wilson for Oil, and Yamada for the Zaibatsu. They actually took the bait." He nudged the corporal.

"Look at them, soldier. Those three fat cats are responsible for the drubbing we've been taking for the last six months. They don't look like much, do they?"

"Some of the men are saying it doesn't take much, sir," replied the corporal flatly, not looking at the screen.

"Is that a fact? Well now it's our turn. Get Command on the phone and tell them the three little pigs are in the briar patch."

• • •

"Can I speak to you a moment, Captain?"

"Certainly, Lieutenant, but it'll have to be quick."

The lieutenant stepped into his CO's office and stood before the desk, fidgeting slightly.

"Well, sir, I think we've got a morale problem on our hands."

"We've had a morale problem for months, Larry. Why should today be any different?"

"It's the executions, sir. There's a lot of bad talk going around the men."

"Were they informed the men executed were infiltrators? Spies for the corporations who've been selling us all out for months?"

"Yes, sir. But . . . well . . . it's the suddenness of it all. This morning they had breakfast with those guys. Then all of a sudden . . . well, a lot of the men think they should have gotten a trial is all."

"Lieutenant, it's been explained—the corporation men have communication devices like we've never seen. They could have had something built into their boots or woven in their uniforms. If we took the time to observe formalities, they could have gotten word out. We couldn't take that chance."

"Well, the men think that without a trial it could have been any one of them. Now they've got the feeling that at any moment they could be pulled out of line and shot without any chance to defend themselves against the charges."

"Damn it, Larry, we know those men were spies. We ran everybody through the computers. Their finances, their families' finances—everybody got checked. You, me, everybody. Those men were on the corporations' payroll, either directly or through a front. We haven't been able to move without those guys tipping the enemy. I don't like it either, but that's the way we had to do it."

"Okay, Captain, I'll try to tell them. . . ."

"Wait a minute, Lieutenant Booth. There's more. I just got the call from HQ. Alert the men to be ready to move out in fifteen minutes. We're mounting an offensive."

"An off . . . but sir, what about the cease-fire?"

The captain leaned back.

"It's all tied in together, Lieutenant. We've got their commanders tied up at the conference tables and their spies are dead. For the first time in this war, we've got a chance to catch those damn mercenaries napping."

"But. . . ."

"Lieutenant, we don't have time to argue. This is coordinated with all the other forces. Our troops are making a world-wide push to try to finish the war in one fell swoop. Now alert the men!"

Wilson was clenching and unclenching his fists nervously out of sight under the table. It was clear to Yamada that the Oiler wanted to speak, but it had been agreed in advance that Yamada would do the talking and Wilson held his peace. As a solid front, the three men sat staring levelly down the table at government representatives facing them, ignoring the guns leveled at them by the guards.

"We cannot help but notice, gentlemen, that there are no civilians in your number." Yamada's voice was, as always, patiently polite.

"Are your governments sanctioning your action or is this a purely military decision?"

The American officer who seemed to be doing the talking for the government forces smiled wickedly as he mimicked Yamada's speech.

"The military is, as always, carrying out the orders of our governments. You may therefore assume that this is the governments' official stance on negotiating a truce with the corporations."

"Then perhaps you could clarify for us what exactly it is you mean when you say we are under arrest?"

"It means you are detained, incommunicado, bagged. It means that we're sick of being blackmailed. We don't bargain with extortionists; we arrest them. When the corporations pull their troops out, we let you go. Until then, you sit here and rot. Only one thing—you don't get a phone call. Your troops will just have to get along without your golden tones."

Even though he kept his face impassive, Yamada's thoughts turned to the transmitter in his belt. By now the news of their arrest would be en route to the home offices . . . and to the mercenaries.

"Your usual, gentlemen?"

The petite waitress smiled fetchingly.

"Only if you'll join us, Tamia," leered the older of the three men seated at the table, beckoning to her.

The girl rolled her eyes in exasperated horror.

"Oh, nooo! If the boss saw me. . . ." She rolled her eyes again. "I'd lose my job like that." She clicked her fingers. "Then where would I work?"

"You could come and live with me."

"Oh!" She giggled and laid a hand on his shoulder. "You're terrible!"

One of the other men leaned forward conspiratorially as she disappeared through the beaded curtains into the kitchen.

"Sir, I don't think it's wise to. . . ."

"Relax, Captain." The older man waved him silent.

"That's why we're in our civvies—so we don't have to keep looking over our shoulders all the time. Nobody recognizes us out of uniform. I've been flirting with that little number for over a month now. Sooner or later she's bound to give in."

"But sir. . . ."

"If anything was going to happen, it would have by now. Look, she doesn't even know my name, so relax."

But Tamia knew his name, and a good deal more. General Thomas Dunn was the main reason she was working at this shabby restaurant, an assignment that ended this evening when she received a phone call. The general stopped here nightly for a bowl of won ton soup, and tonight there would be a special surprise in it. Tonight she would include the special noodles she had been carrying for a month.

Actually, the basis for the idea was Eskimo, not Japanese, but the Japanese were never a group to ignore a good idea just because someone else thought of it first. The Eskimos would kill polar bears by freezing coiled slivers of bone inside a snowball flavored with seal blubber and leaving it on the ice floes. A bear would eat the snowball, and his body heat would melt the snow, releasing the bone sliver to tear at his insides.

The Japanese had improved on the concept. Instead of bone slivers, they were using a substance more like ground glass, guaranteed to cause a painful and irreversible death. In addition, they added a special touch of subtlety especially for the general. Instead of ice and seal blubber, they imbedded their lethal surprise in a special gel. Tamia would serve the general and his aides out of the same large bowl openly at the table. The gel would pass completely through the human digestive tract without dissolving. In fact, it would only dissolve if it came into contact with alcohol.

The files on the government forces were very complete. Of the three men at the table, only the general drank. In fact, he always had at least one nightcap before retiring for the evening.

After his death, his aides could and would tell the medic that they had shared the general's soup without any noticeable side effects, averting suspicion from the small restaurant and from Tamia.

Tamia scowled as she went about her task. While it was true she was successfully completing her mission and it would look good on her performance review, she wished she was in the field with the rest of her team. That's where the challenging work was.

Lieutenant Booth was nervous. So far their "big offensive" had been no different from a hundred other fruitless missions they had been on. All their infrared and sonic scans had yielded nothing. They were sweeping back and forth looking for one of the laser cannons reported to be in their vicinity. In theory, if they could knock out the cannon and if the other forces were equally successful, the government troops could regain air supremacy.

That was the theory. In actuality, they were finding nothing to fight. It was the lieutenant's guess
that this mission would end up like all the others—a big bust. The only difference was that their
radios were acting up again. They had lost contact
both with headquarters and with their flanking company.

This was nothing new. It wasn't the first time they
had had trouble with their radios in the field. As such,
the captain just kept the company plodding on, but
it made Booth nervous. To him it meant their much
valued technology was unreliable. If the radios could
malfunction, so could the scanners!

" . . . And I repeat, gentlemen, the troops employed
by the corporations have not been fighting at their
full capacity."

"Frankly, Mr. Yamada, I find that a little hard to
swallow."

Yamada sighed slightly.

"For proof, I would offer two examples. First, it
is not in the corporations' best interests to indulge
in the bloodbath form of warfare the governments'
forces seem to favor. We make a living by selling our
products to consumers, to the public. If we inflict
heavy casualties on you, it hurts us in the market-
place. Currently, public sympathy, as well as the
sympathy of many of your own troops, is with the
corporations. We will not jeopardize this by making
martyrs out of the forces opposing us. All we have
to do is wait until public opinion forces your governments to withdraw from the conflict."

The military men in the room maintained a
thoughtful silence as Yamada pursued his point.

"Think back, gentlemen. Our troops have spent exceptional time and effort evading your forces. When they have fought, it has always been to discourage rather than to destroy. In every situation, your troops were called upon to surrender or withdraw before our men opened fire."

The American officer was scowling.

"You mentioned two points of proof, Mr. Yamada. What's the other one?"

"There may be those who would question our capacities, whether we have the ability to inflict more damage than we have. To prove this ability, you need only to try to phone your commanding officers. I say specifically to phone because by now we will have jammed or disrupted all your radio communications. As soon as you placed us under arrest, an order went out to some very specialized soldiers in our employment. All officers in your forces above the rank of lieutenant colonel have been assassinated. Your forces, already demoralized, are now without communications or leaders."

Lieutenant Booth could scarcely contain his excitement as he waited for confirmation on the smoke flare coordinates.

"I've got it, Lieutenant! Right on the button! They're clear!"

"Open fire! Level the entire target area."

The shells were hitting before he stopped talking as his mortar teams eagerly pumped round after round into the designated target area.

At last! After six months—contact! He watched gleefully as explosion after explosion rocked the area. Luckily they picked up that transmission from B

Company. The way the radios had been acting up they could have missed it completely. Probably some new jamming device the mercenaries were using. Well, it was nice to know they had trouble with their gear too.

"Keep it up, men!"

B Company was under fire from the mercenaries. If the radio signal hadn't come through the bastards could have chopped up the government troops one company at a time, but now their plan had backfired. B Company's position was marked by the smoke flare, and for the first time the mortar teams knew where the mercenaries were.

"Lieutenant Booth! Cease fire! Cease fire!"

The lieutenant turned to see a soldier running toward him waving his arms.

"Cease fire!" he barked at his men, and the cry was echoed down the line.

The sergeant who had hailed him ran up, ashen-faced and out of breath.

"What is it, Sergeant?" Booth was aware of the nearby teams listening in curiously.

"Lieutenant, that's not . . . we saw them . . . it's not . . ."

"Spit it out, Sergeant!"

"It's not the mercenaries. We're shelling our own troops!"

"What?"

"Sommers climbed a tree with binoculars to watch the show! Those are our men down there!"

"But the smoke flare. . . ."

Realization struck him like a slap in the face. It was the mercenaries. They had given him a fake radio call and a fake smoke flare.

He suddenly was aware of his men moving. They were abandoning their equipment and walking back toward the base. Their eyes were glazed and some of them were crying. He knew he should call to them, order them, console them. He knew that he should, but he couldn't.

" . . . Now look, Yamada. We're through playing around. You've got fifteen minutes to make up your mind. Either you and your playmates call off your dogs or we'll have a few assassinations of our own here and now!"

Yamada considered them levelly.

"Gentlemen, you seem to have missed the point completely. First, holding us hostage will gain you nothing. Terrorist groups have been kidnapping corporation executives for over twenty-five years now, asking either for money or special considerations. In all that time, the corporations' policy for dealing with them has not changed. We don't make deals, and the executive threatened is on his own."

He crossed his arms and continued.

"Secondly, you assume that you can threaten us into selling out our forces in exchange for our lives. We are as dedicated to our cause as any soldier and as such, are ready to sacrifice our lives if need be. I do not expect you gentlemen to believe this on the strength of my words—it must be demonstrated."

He raised his right hand and pointed to his left bicep.

"In the lining of my coat was an ampule of poison. As I crossed my arms, I injected it into my bloodstream. I am neither afraid to die nor am I willing to serve as your hostage."

He blinked as if trying to clear his focus.

"Mr. Becker, I fear you will have to. . . ."

His face hit the table, but he didn't feel it. The other two corporation men did not look at his body, but continued staring down the table at the military men who were sitting in stunned silence.

"I feel Mr. Yamada has stated our position adequately," Becker intoned. "And I for one do not feel like continuing this discussion."

He rose, Wilson following suit.

"We're leaving now, gentlemen. Shoot if you feel it will do any good."

23

"THIS STILL SEEMS STRANGE."

"What does?" Judy turned from gazing out the taxi window to direct her attention to him.

"Dictating terms to the government. It's weird. I mean, as long as I've been working, the corporations have bitched about government controls and chafed under the rules. Sometimes we bought our way into some favorable lesiglation and sometimes we just moved our operations to a more favorable climate. But just telling them . . . that's weird."

"Look at it like the Magna Carta."

"The which?"

"History . . . medieval Europe. A bunch of the lorded barons, the fat cats of the era, got together and forced the king to sign a document giving them a voice in government."

"Is that what we're doing?"

"In a manner of speaking. Look, love, any system of government involves voluntary acceptance of that authority. Once the populace decides they don't want to play along, the Lord High Muckity-Mucks are out of luck."

"Except in a communist police state."

"Including a communist police state. If the people aren't happy or at least content, they're going to take things into their own hands and trample you."

"But if anyone mouths off you can just take them out and shoot them."

"If enough people are upset, you're in trouble. You can't shoot them all. And who's going to do the shooting? If things are out of hand, odds are the military won't follow your lead either."

"It still seems unnatural."

"It's the most natural thing in the world. Ignore governments for a minute. Look at any power structure. Look at the beginning of the unions. The fat cats had all the cards. It was their football. But when conditions got bad enough, the workers damn well dealt themselves in whether the fat cats liked it or not."

"But the unions are only a minor power now."

"Right, because they're no longer necessary. Business finally wised up to the fact that keeping the workers happy is the key to success. The conditions that caused the unions to form and justified their existence disappeared, and people started wondering what they were paying their dues for. Just like the corporations are asking what they're paying taxes for. You can't force a loyalty to any system. It's either there or it isn't. Inertia maintains the status quo, but once the tide turns there is no stopping it."

"You make this sound like a take-over."

"Effectively it is. The only reason the governments still exist today is because they do a lot of scut work the corporations don't want to dirty their hands with. But anything we want, we've got. They tried to assert their authority and proved that they don't have any."

"So where do we go from here?"

"We go in there." She pointed through the window at the large steel and glass building as the taxi pulled over to the curb. "As delegates to the First United Negotiations Council, the most powerful assemblage the free world has ever seen—every major corporation and industrial group gathered to decide how we want the world to run."

As they started up the stairs, she drew close to him.

"Stay close to me, huh?"

"Nervous? After that talk in the car, I thought you were ready to take on anyone in the council."

"It's not the council, it's them."

She nodded at the mercenaries lounging around the lobby, their hard eyes betraying the casual manner with which they checked the delegates' ID's.

"Them? C'mon, sweetheart, those are our heroes; without them, where would we be now?"

"I still don't like them; they're animals."

She quickened her step, and Fred had to hurry to keep up.

"How about that?"

"What?" Tidwell drifted over to the mezzanine railing to see what Clancy was ogling.

"That little bit of fluff with the old geezer—rough life, huh?"

"Nice to know what our fighting is for, isn't it—so some fat cat can bring his chippie along to meetings with him."

"Don't short-sell them, Steve. They fight as hard as we do. Just in different ways."

"I suppose." Tidwell turned away and lit another cigarette, leaning back against the railing.

"What's eating you today, Steve? You seem kinda on edge?"

"I dunno. I keep getting the feeling something's about to happen."

"What?"

"I dunno. Maybe it's just nerves. I'm not used to just standing around."

"Just the wind-down after being in the field so long. You'll get over it."

They stood in silence for a few moments. Then Tidwell eased off the railing, and ground out his cigarette in an ashtray.

"Clancy, what do you know about samurai?"

"Not much. They were bad-ass fighters as individuals, but not much as an army."

"Do you know what happened to them?"

"No. Outmoded when gunpowder came in, I guess."

"Wrong—they got done in by a change in the system."

"How's that?"

"Well, they were professional bodyguards when Japan was essentially a bunch of small countries each lorded over by a warlord. Anyone who was wealthy and landed maintained a brace of samurai to keep his neighbors from taking it all away from him. The constant raiding and feuds kept them busy for quite a few generations. Then the country became united under one emperor who extended his protection over the whole shebang. All of a sudden the samurai were unnecessary and expensive, the clans were disbanded, and they were reduced to beggars and outlaws."

"And you're worried about that happening to us?"

"It's a possibility."

"There are other options."

"Such as?"

"Well, for openers. . . ."

"Wait a minute." Tidwell was suddenly alert and moving along the railing. A group of some twenty mercenaries had just entered and were standing just inside the glass doors.

"Who are those men?" Tidwell leaned on the railing and craned his neck, trying to see a familiar face in the group.

"They're our relief."

"Relief? What relief? We're supposed to be on guard for another. . . ." He stopped abruptly.

Clancy was holding his favorite derringer leveled at him, the bore immense when viewed from the front.

"What's this?"

"It'll all be clear in a few minutes. In the meantime, just take my word that those men are here with peaceful intentions."

"Who are they?"

"Some of the guys from my old outfit."

"Your old outfit? You mean during. . . ."

"During the Russo-Chinese War, right. The C-Block is about to break their communications silence, and we're delivering the message."

"Since when did you work for the C-Block?"

"Never stopped."

"I see. Well, now what?"

"Now you tell the guards they're relieved. Tell 'em it's bonus time off or something, but make it sound natural. My men have been briefed on you and your team and will be watching for anything out of line."

"I thought you said this was peaceful."

"It is, but we don't want anyone going off half-cocked before we have our say."

"So all I have to do is dismiss the men."

"Right. But stick around. I think you'll find this kinda interesting."

"Wouldn't miss it for the world."

If Fred had not been already bored with the opening comments from the chairman pro tem, he probably would not have noticed the mercenaries entering the auditorium, but curiosity made him watch first leisurely, then with growing interest as the patterns formed. Four of them spreading quietly along the back walkway. Three more appearing in the balcony. Fred straightened slightly. Were the two by the door holding weapons on the stone-faced mercenary leaning against the back wall?

Something was up. What was it? Had an assassin been infiltrated into the meeting? A bomb threat?

Fred's eyes scanned the assemblage uneasily. His eyes met those of the stone-faced mercenary in the back who arched one eyebrow in surprise, then slowly and solemnly winked at him.

What was up? Oh, well, they'd know soon enough. One of the mercenaries flanked by two others was approaching the podium. The chairman noted their approach and interrupted his speech. He stepped down and spoke briefly with the center mercenary. The delegates took advantage of the interruption to converse and shift back and forth. Fred watched the conversation. It seemed to be growing more heated. Suddenly the chairman broke away shaking his head angrily and started back for the podium. The mercenary he had been talking to gestured to one of his flankers. The man stepped in behind the chairman and chopped him across the back of the neck with his hand. The chairman crumpled to the floor.

Jesus Christ! What was going on? The delegates recoiled in horror as the mercenary dragged the chairman to a vacant seat where they deposited him in an unceremonious heap, then turned to face the assemblage. As their apparent leader took over the podium, the audience sank into silence.

"Well, folks, it looks like I'm going to have to do this without an introduction."

He paused as if expecting a laugh. There was only silence as the delegates watched him coldly.

"Some of you may recognize me as one of your mercenaries. We have a proposal to put before the council and. . . ."

"What the hell is this?"

A voice rang out from the audience, which was quickly echoed by several other indignant delegates. Clancy raised his hand, and suddenly the other mercenaries were moving into position along the edge of the room, drawing their weapons as they went. The assemblage suddenly submerged into silence once more.

"I do apologize for the unorthodox nature of this presentation, but I'll have to ask that you hear me out before any questions are raised. What is more, I'll have to ask you to listen quietly and not make any sudden outbursts or movements. The boys are a little jumpy and we wouldn't want them to think you were getting hostile when you really weren't."

Fred shot a glance back at the stern-faced mercenary who shrugged as if to say he didn't know what was happening either.

"Now, as I was starting to say, we are a coalition of mercenaries. Our current employers are the people you refer to as the C-Block."

Fred felt his flesh turn cold. Commies! They were being held at gunpoint by a pack of Commies!

"We are relaying a proposal to you from our employers. What we are offering you is a lasting world peace. Now let me elaborate on that before everyone panics. In the past, when someone offers world peace, it's usually on their terms. 'Do things my way and nobody will get hurt!' Well, this isn't what we're saying. We aren't saying the free world should convert to communism, or that the Communists should go imperialistic. We are proposing a method by which both ideals can be left free to pattern their lives according to the dictates of their conscience and traditions."

Neat trick if you can do it. Fred was nonetheless interested.

"One of the purposes of this Council is to determine how much support you feel you should give the governments in the way of taxes. Part and parcel with this is an appraisal of how much they really need. We would suggest that the governments of the world can cut a major portion of their expense by disbanding their armed forces."

A murmur rippled through the delegates which quickly subsided as they remembered they were under the guns.

"What we propose to replace the multitude of individual armies with is one worldwide army of hard-core professionals, mercenaries if you will, paid equally by the corporations and the C-Block. It would be their job to maintain world peace, moving to block any country or group who attempted a forceful infringement on their neighbors. This was tried unsuccessfully once by the United Nations. It failed for two reasons. First, the nations still kept their armed forces, giving them a capacity for attacking each other; and second, the UN forces were not given adequate power to do their job. May I assure the assemblage that if we say we will stop a conflict, it will be stopped."

He smiled grimly at them. Not a person in the room doubted him.

"Now, there are several automatic objections which would be raised to such a force. The most obvious is the fear of a military takeover. In reply, I would point out that right now we could kill everyone in this room. The question is why? Any such army which abused its power would rapidly be confronted by several things. The first would be an armed uprising of the general populace. If every time we killed someone, five other people got upset and we had to kill them, eventually there would be no one left in the world but soldiers. We are not that kind of madmen. By definition, we are soldiers, not farmers or storekeepers. We are dependent on you for our livelihood. You don't kill the goose that lays the golden egg, and a sane man doesn't shoot his boss."

He paused. There was a thoughtful silence in the room.

"It might be pointed out that we have been operating in the C-Block for a number of years now in this capacity. They needed all available manpower for their rebuilding, so they cannibalized the army and turned the job of security over to us. It was a desperation move, but it's worked. The arrangement has proven beneficial to all concerned. I might add that to date there have been no attempted military takeovers. The only lingering fear is of a takeover attempt from outside the C-Block, which is why we are here. We offer you a cheap and lasting peace by subscribing to our services. There is no threat of invasion if there is no armed, organized invasion force."

His words hung in the air. Fred found himself trying to imagine a world without a threat of war.

"There is another, less pleasant objection which might be raised to this plan. I'm sure that as businessmen, it has occurred to you. War is good business. It can provide a vital shot in the arm to a sagging economy. Do we really want to eliminate war?

"Before I answer that question, let me point out another problem. How do we keep in training? If we are successful, if war becomes obsolete, if there is no enemy for us to train for, what is to keep us from becoming fat, lazy, and useless leeches?"

He smiled at the room.

"You in this room have given us an answer to both problems. For the last two years in the C-Block, we have been using your kill-suits in our training. Our main purpose was to provide hard training for our troops, but it had a surprising side product. Military maneuvers in kill-suits have emerged as a spectator sport of astounding popularity. We have developed various categories of competition and regular teams have formed, each with their followers and fans. Apparently, once the populace becomes accustomed to the fact that no real injuries or deaths are incurred, they find it far more enjoyable than movies or television. Certain of our mercenaries have become minor celebrities and occasionally have to be guarded from autograph-seeking fans."

There was a low buzz of conversation going as he continued.

"Now this means that not only does the military industry continue, but that there is an unexpected windfall of a new spectator sport. I am sure I do not have to elaborate for this assemblage the profits latent in proper handling of a spectator sport."

This time he actually got a low ripple of laughter in response to his joke. Even Fred found himself chortling. Don't teach your grandmother to steal sheep, sonny.

"Well, I feel I have used up enough of your time on the proposal. I'd ask that you discuss it among yourselves and with your superiors. We will be back in a week, at which time we will be ready to answer any and all questions you might have. I would like to apologize for the tactic of holding you at gunpoint, but we were not certain what your initial reaction would be to our appearance. I will pay you the compliment of telling you the guns are loaded. We are more than slightly afraid of you. You are dangerous men. Thank you."

He stepped down from the podium and started for the door, gathering his men as he went.

Gutsy bastard! thought Fred, and started to clap. Others picked it up, and by the time the mercenaries reached the door, the applause was thunderous. They paused, waved, and left.

"Sorry I couldn't tell you sooner, Steve, but orders are orders."

"No problem."

"I want to tell you I rate drawing down on you as one of the nerviest things I've done in my life. Oh, I have a contract offer for you from the coalition."

"Kind of hoped you would. Come on, I'll buy you a drink."

"Hey, thanks. I need one after that."

They walked on in silence for a while. Finally Tidwell broke the reverie.

"Autograph-seeking fans?"

"Hey, wait till it happens to you. It's spooky."

They both laughed.

"Say, tell me, Clancy—what's it like working for the C-Block?"

"Do you want the truth? I couldn't say this back there for fear of being torn apart, but there's no difference. Call it the United Board of Directors or the Party. A fat cat string-puller is a fat cat string-puller, and anyone in a position of power without controls has the same problems. The phrasing is different, but they both say the same thing. Keep the workers happy with an illusion of having some say so they don't tear us out of our cushy pigeonholes. That's what makes our job so easy. People are people. They shy away from violence and stuff their faces with free candy whenever they can. And nobody but nobody acknowledges their base drives like greed. We do, so we have the world by the short and curlys."

Tidwell waved a hand.

"That's too heavy for me. Speaking of base drives, I still want that drink. Where are we going?"

"Aki's found a little Japanese restaurant that serves a good Irish whiskey. The whole crew hangs out there."

"You're on. Autograph-seeking fans, huh?"

The two mercenaries walked on, laughing, oblivious to the curious and indignant stares directed at them.

24

THOMAS MAUSIER WAS EXTREMELY BUSY.
Ever since the C-Block's curtain of silence had been
lifted, his business had almost tripled. All the questions that had backlogged so long without answers
were suddenly live again. His agents were having a
field day.

The biggest problem confronting Mausier currently was determining if this was merely a wave that
would die back down to normal levels, or if he should
expand his operations to handle the new volume. He
had already had to add a second shift just to process
the items pouring in 'round the clock, and he hadn't
had time to pursue his hobby in nearly a month. Not
bad for a little business he had started to escape the
gray flannel rat race.

At one point he had been worried about his business collapsing in the wake of the new order, but
he should have known better. Information doesn't

answer questions, it raises new ones. As long as there was money and people at stake, he'd be in business.

The light on the closed circuit television screen on his desk glowed to life, and he keyed it on.

"Yes, Ms. Witley?"

"Two men in the outer office to see you. They say it's important."

As she spoke, she subtly manipulated the controls and the two men appeared in a split-screen effect.

They looked like corporate types, and their visit was uncomfortably close to lunch. Then he remembered his first visit from Hornsby.

"Bring them back."

A few moments later they appeared. Ms. Witley did a quick round of introductions and left. Mausier slyly tripped the videotape recorders as he shook their hands. He'd gotten into the habit of taping all of his private conferences for later review.

"Now then Mr. Stills, Mr. Weaver. Are you buying or selling?"

They looked at him blankly. He felt a spark of annoyance.

"Buying or selling . . . ?"

"Information. I assume that's why you're here. We don't deal in anything else."

"Oh! No! I'm afraid you've got the wrong idea about why we're here. You see, Mr. Weaver and myself are here representing the United Board of Corporations."

Mausier suddenly thought of his gun. It was at home, hanging in the bedroom closet. He hadn't worn it in weeks.

"I don't understand, gentlemen. Is there some kind of complaint. . . ."

"No, no. Quite the contrary." Stills's smile was pleasant and reassuring. "There's a matter we'd like to discuss with you that we feel is of mutual benefit. We were hoping you'd let us buy you lunch and we could talk at leisure."

Mausier didn't return his smile.

"I'm in the habit of working through lunch. One of the disadvantages of working for yourself is that, unlike the corporations, there *is* such a thing as an indispensable man. In this business it's me. Now if you could state your business, I am rather a busy man."

The two men exchanged glances and shrugged without moving their shoulders.

"Very well. We are authorized by the Board to speak to you about selling out—that is, the corporations are interested in acquiring your business."

Mausier was stunned. For a moment he was unable to speak.

"Frankly, I think the first way you phrased it was more accurate," he blurted out at last.

Weaver smiled, but Stills held up a restraining hand.

"Seriously, I phrased that rather poorly. Let me try again. You see, the Board has been investigating your operation for some time. The more they find, the more impressed they are."

Mausier inclined his head slightly at the compliment.

"Originally, the plan was to build a similar operation for the Board's use. As it turned out, the more they looked into it, the more they realized the difficulties of duplicating your setup. Just building the network of agents you have would take time, and during that time, important things could happen."

He paused to light a cigarette. Mausier glanced at his equipment but said nothing.

"So anyway, they decided the most efficient way to approach the problem was to simply acquire your setup and put it to work for them."

"There's one major drawback to that plan," Mausier interrupted. "I'm not interested in selling."

Again Stills held up his hand.

"Now, don't jump to conclusions, Mr. Mausier. I don't think you completely understand what we're proposing. You'd still be in control of the operation. You'd still be carried on the payroll at a hefty salary in addition, of course, to the acquisitions price, which I'll admit I feel is exorbitant. We wouldn't be taking anything away from you; in fact, we're anticipating—we're expecting the operation will expand. With proper pressure, all the corporations will deal through you for information. The way it's looking, you could end up as one of the most powerful men in the corporate world."

This time it was Mausier who interrupted, rising to his feet and leaning across his desk.

"And I don't think *you* understand, gentlemen. I don't want to be one of the most powerful men in the corporate world. I don't want to expand my operation. And I don't want to sell my business!"

He was getting excited and losing control, but for once he didn't care.

"I spent enough time in your corporate world to know the one thing I wanted from it was out. I don't like brown-nosing, I don't like operating plans, I don't like performance reviews, I don't like benefits packages, I don't like pointless meetings, I don't like employee newspapers, I don't like office gossip, and I don't like being expendable. In short, gentlemen, I don't like corporations. That's why I started this business. To run it, I work harder than both of you put together and probably make less. But there's one thing I am that I'll bet neither of you has the vaguest conception of—I'm happy. You can't tax it, but it means a lot to me. Do I make myself quite clear?"

The two men languished in their chairs, apparently unmoved by his tirade.

"I don't think you understand, Mausier," said Stills softly. "We weren't asking you!"

Mausier suddenly felt cold. He sank slowly back into his chair as Stills continued.

"Now, we're being nice and giving you an honest deal, but don't kid yourself about having a choice. In case you haven't been following the news, the corporations are running things now. When they say 'jump,' you don't say 'how high?' You say 'Can I come down now?' That's the way it is whether you like it or not."

Mausier felt weak.

"And if I don't jump?" he asked quietly.

Stills grimaced.

"Now that would be unpleasant for everybody."

Mausier raised his eyes to look at them.

"Are you saying they'd actually kill me?"

Stills actually looked surprised.

"Kill you? Hell, man, you read too many spy novels!"

Weaver spoke for the first time.

"Look around you, Mr. Mausier. You're running a very delicate operation here. What happens to it if the phone company refused you service? Or if the people who manufacture all the gadgetry either recall it or refuse to service it? The Zaibatsu have been monitoring your scramblers for years. Suppose they publish a notice in all newspapers that in one week they'll publish a list of names of all agents still on your list of clients? Now, I don't like threats, Mr. Mausier, but if we wanted to we could shut you down overnight."

Mausier sagged in his chair. The two corporate men waited in respectful silence for him to recover his composure.

"Where do we go from here?"

Stills stood up.

"I've got to report in. Weaver here will stay with you as your new assistant to start learning the ropes. Policy says that all key personnel are supposed to have understudies."

He started for the door.

"Stills!"

Mausier's voice stopped him with his hand on the knob.

"Is this the way it's going to be?"

Stills shrugged and smiled and left without answering.

The room lapsed into silence as Mausier sat staring into space. Suddenly, he felt a hand on his shoulder. It was Weaver.

"Cheer up, Mr. Mausier." His voice was sympathetic. "It could be worse. You're a valuable man. Just play ball and they'll take care of you. You know, 'go along, get along.' "

Mausier didn't respond. He just kept thinking about the gun in his bedroom closet.